Well, Karl's a creep, that's for sure, Phoebe decided. *But a demon? Hard to say . . .*

Jessica eased back as Craig walked by, sighing as she took in the view. She wasn't the only one. Paige and Craig were exchanging very knowing glances.

The breathtaking and reportedly harmless streaks of light crept closer, and Phoebe backed away from the brilliant shards of rainbow illuminating the room. Something about the lovely gleaming streaks of brilliance disturbed her in ways she couldn't put into words.

Suddenly, something warm and furry scampered against the back of her ankle. She turned, twisted, and yelped in surprise. A tiny black form burst into view, then disappeared behind the couch.

A cat? Phoebe thought, remembering the gigantic grooves in the door upstairs. *What—*

Charmed®

The Book of Three: The Official Companion to the Hit Show

Seasons of the Witch, Vol. 1

The Warren Witches

The Power of Three

Kiss of Darkness

The Crimson Spell

Whispers from the Past

Voodoo Moon

Haunted by Desire

The Gypsy Enchantment

The Legacy of Merlin

Soul of the Bride

Beware What You Wish

Charmed Again

Spirit of the Wolf

Garden of Evil

Date with Death

Dark Vengeance

Shadow of the Sphinx

Something Wiccan This Way Comes

Mist and Stone

Mirror Image

Between Worlds

Truth and Consequences

Luck Be a Lady

Inherit the Witch

A Tale of Two Pipers

The Brewing Storm

Survival of the Fittest

Pied Piper

Mystic Knoll

Changeling Places

The Queen's Curse

Picture Perfect

Demon Doppelgangers

Hurricane Hex

As Puck Would Have It

Sweet Talkin' Demon

Light of the World

House of Shards

Phoebe Who?

High Spirits

Published by Simon & Schuster

HIGH SPIRITS

HIGH SPIRITS

An original novel by Scott Ciencin

Based on the hit TV series created by

Constance M. Burge

SIMON SPOTLIGHT ENTERTAINMENT
New York   London   Toronto   Sydney

To my beloved wife, Denise

S|S|E

SIMON SPOTLIGHT ENTERTAINMENT
An imprint of Simon & Schuster Children's Publishing Division
1230 Avenue of the Americas, New York, New York 10020
® and © 2007 Spelling Television Inc. A CBS Company. All Rights Reserved.
All rights reserved, including the right of reproduction in whole or in part in any form.
SIMON SPOTLIGHT ENTERTAINMENT and related logo are trademarks of Simon & Schuster, Inc.
Manufactured in the United States of America
First Edition 10 9 8 7 6 5 4 3 2 1
Library of Congress Control Number 2006933762
ISBN-13: 978-1-4169-3668-8
ISBN-10: 1-4169-3668-8

Prologue

Hollywood, 1926

Robert Maxwell, star of stage and screen, grinned, waved, and drove himself ahead on the red carpet as blinding flashes from cameras exploded in his eyes and glass from exploded flashbulbs crunched under his expensive Italian loafers. Spotlights streaked through the night sky above the Egyptian Theater on Hollywood Boulevard, the first and greatest movie theater in Los Angeles, for the premiere of Maxwell's latest, *The Pirate King!*

Just a few feet ahead, Maxwell spotted a strapping young actor wearing the costume of an Egyptian guard prowl menacingly across the roof's parapet, ready to call out the start of the evening's performance. He was getting close to the theater's entrance—heralded by massive wide pillars—and an end to smiling for the press.

This premiere was a toned-down affair, all things considered. Maxwell requested that there be no live orchestra or death-defying descent from the heavens by parachutists. The actor had not felt like his old show-boaty self this week and he wished to fulfill this work obligation with as little fuss and muss as possible. He even broke his industry-wide tradition of wearing his costume and wig from the film—to the dissatisfaction of the paparazzi.

Maxwell remembered how excited he'd been when he first saw this place. *Robin Hood*, starring Fairbanks himself, had been the first world premiere at this theater back in '22, and the theater's design had been inspired by the discovery that year of King Tut's tomb.

The stars shone down from the evening sky and a gentle breeze brushed at his neck, tickling the hairs at his nape. The itch suddenly stole around his collar like playful fingers, and he wanted to scratch it but he couldn't. His every move was being scrutinized by the press, and he knew the motion would show up in photographs and make him look uncomfortable in his suit: which he was, but he couldn't very well let that on, now could he?

What in heaven's name is a farm boy from Nebraska like me doing here? Maxwell wondered for perhaps the thousandth time this year. *When are they going to realize their mistake and take back the millions they've paid me and the awards they've handed out like candy—all for traipsing about before the cameras like the hammy goof that I am? Even the*

Royal Shakespeare Company has allowed me to per-
form with them. Madness, sheer madness . . .

Three of the greatest names in the motion picture business were pressing in on him from
behind, and a wily, gray-haired gentleman who
owned the biggest film studio on the planet was
two steps ahead of him. In front of them was his
female costar, stunning in her beaded satin
evening dress topped by a cut-velvet jacket.
Maxwell knew that he, too, was considered
"Hollywood royalty," and that idea made him
smile all the more. He was forty-two years old,
handsome, and just this side of "distinguished."
At this rate, he would never have to grow up.

Ah, but make-believe is so much fun . . . so much
better than real life!

"Mr. Maxwell!" a reporter called. "Robert!"

Whirling as he heard his name, Maxwell
wondered if his grimace would truly register as
an inviting smile. He knew that it would, of
course. He had seen himself in the news enough
times to no longer worry about such things.
Besides, he had more important matters on his
mind these days.

A pretty brunette thrust a notepad his way.
"Is it true that you turned down the leads in no
less than three major upcoming films so that you
can take a spiritual retreat to Tibet?"

Interesting, he thought, fighting back the urge
to swallow hard in panic. *That had to be more than
just a lucky guess. . . .*

The actor turned to the battery of reporters and brandished his dazzling smile. "I think you're getting confused with my charitable work in Africa and other impoverished countries. Certainly it involves a good deal of travel, but that's small sacrifice for trying to make a difference in this world."

He watched them nod and quickly jot down notes, though few had seemed particularly enthused over his answer. Taking the high road rarely sold newspapers. If he didn't add something quickly, they would swarm all over him about the Tibetan journey. But he knew what to do: Scandal was always an irresistible lure.

With a wink, he added, "Now if you had asked which of the many starlets I've been seeing recently might be joining me in my purely altruistic ventures, particularly those who are still *technically* married . . ."

The gaggle of ravenous reporters exploded with excitement as they pushed at the red ropes rigged to hold them back. Police officers and security men pressed up against them, reducing them to a surging storm of thrusting hands, flashing cameras, and frantic cries.

"No, no, I've probably said too much already," Maxwell noted reproachfully as he allowed himself to be led into the theater.

By midnight he was back at his sprawling mansion nestled high in the Hollywood hills, sipping a margarita by the pool. He gestured for his manservant and driver, Gino, who sauntered over.

"Gino, do you know of anyone on the staff who isn't happy working here for me? Or anyone who might be in trouble where money is concerned?"

Gino scratched at his thick black mustache and shrugged. "Times can be tight out there, it's true, boss. But I can't think of anyone who's gotten in too deep or has an ax to grind with you. I've worked a lot of places, for a lot of folks, and you're the best boss I ever had. Everybody here feels that way."

"Thanks, Gino," Maxwell said with his million-dollar smile. "You're a good egg."

Gino's swarthy Latin face lit up. "Thanks, boss!"

Maxwell settled back on his bamboo pool chair, his brow knitting with concern. He ran the incident at the premiere over and over in his mind as if he were in the screening room and the footage were on an endless loop.

He had known that it was only a matter of time before someone at the studio leaked that he had turned down the sequel to *The Thief of Bagdad* and those other two, *Wings* and *The Jazz Singer*. All three projects had astounding scripts and wonderful talent attached, but Maxwell felt he had to focus his attentions elsewhere. *Who would have told the press about his secret trip to*

Tibet? Who among his staff actually knew that—

"Yoo-hoo!" cried a young high-spirited female voice. "I've got a singing telegram just for you!"

Maxwell sat up in surprise as a lovely young woman wearing a scandalous—but quite pleasing to behold—low-cut silver-and-gold two-piece number struggled to keep her balance as she stalked the outer edge of the pool in spike heels. Her cute and smiling pixielike face was wreathed by a platinum blond pageboy bob, and marred by just a touch too much makeup, as if she were not familiar with the fine art of applying it. Still, her proposal tickled him.

A singing telegram? he thought. *What a novel idea!*

Then he recalled hearing a few of the background actors on his last film chitchatting about something of the kind. It seemed that small messenger services were trying out all manners of gimmick to compete with Western Union, but it was, of course, only a matter of time before the idea was appropriated by the larger services.

Moving far too quickly on lean and pleasing muscular legs, the young woman wobbled over his way much like a fawn taking her first steps. With a pretty and oh-so-perky pout, she drew in a sharp breath and squeaked as one of her heels turned over and her lithe form leaped toward the sparkling pool.

Maxwell bolted off his chair and caught her

in his arms an instant before she would have fallen face-first into the water. Her warm hands gripped his rippling biceps as she feebly attempted to steady herself in her broken shoe.

"That's a lost cause, I'm afraid," Maxwell told her. "Walking in heels like that is a risky proposition unless you're used to them."

The girl's eyes were dark and dreamy as she gazed up at her rescuer. With a sigh, he helped her to sit down on the pool chair. She *didn't* let go of his powerful arms. Her body snuggled close and her face nestled against his chest as she peered up at him in abject adoration.

"Who let you in?" he asked.

"Um . . . the gate was open," she murmured.

Maxwell frowned. He'd seen "starstruck" expressions before, and they always looked just like this one. And frankly, without wishing to be unkind to this poor girl, such things bored him. When Robert Maxwell peered into the mirror, he could find no reason why millions should adore the face that stared back at him. He firmly believed that his loving fans were in love with the illusion of who and what he was supposed to be as a Hollywood icon, not the flesh-and-blood man with all the hopes, dreams, and problems of anyone else.

Of course, he was wealthy, but money and "power" were fleeting and entirely useless in the face of certain other issues that served as the great equalizers of all mankind. . . .

Gino came rushing out. "Boss, what's happening? Hey, what's going on here—you want I should get rid of the frail?"

Maxwell smiled up at his friend. "That's okay, Gino. I'll handle things from here. Be seeing you!"

Gino laughed and said, "Not if I see you first." With that, Gino disappeared into the great house. Seconds later, a curtain in the study wavered and kept moving slightly as a shadowy form nestled behind it.

"He's very protective of you," the young woman said, her gaze on that curtained window. "Much more so than someone who's just doing his job."

"You can tell that?" Maxwell asked.

"He's still watching us," she said, nodding to the window. "See, I'm what they call 'powerfully observant.' I don't miss a trick!"

"And who would 'they' be?" asked Maxwell as he caught Gino keeping a watchful eye on them. When he looked back at the woman, she was gazing up at him again, a pout on her pretty face. He laughed. "Because 'they' clearly know of what they speak!"

With a tiny murmur of embarrassment, the young woman eased back from the actor and brought her foot up. She unstrapped the broken shoe and wriggled out of its mate.

Maxwell watched her, smiling gently. He had no idea what his visitor's message really was, but he welcomed the distraction. And Gino was nearby, keeping an eye on things. *She's probably just another actress looking for a leg up in the business*, he reasoned, *and, well, I couldn't help but notice, she really does have nice legs.*

"So what's your message for me on this fine night, upon the dreaded witching hour?" he asked theatrically. He grinned. "Isn't that what they call midnight? The witching hour?"

Her eyes widened, then darted frantically. "I have a very special message for you," the young lady said. "One that can't just be told. It has to be sung."

All right, she wants to be a singer, thought Maxwell. *And it is well-known that I can carry a tune. Perhaps I'll join in. If she's any good at all, I will indeed reward her. It's wonderful to have my mind taken off things, if only for a short time. . . .*

The young woman stood, appearing infinitely more graceful and composed than before. *Perhaps she wasn't a klutz at all, perhaps—*

She wailed as her feet slipped on a wet water slick next to the chair. Her arms pinwheeled, and this time she *did* flop into the pool. Maxwell dove in after her, his hands again settling on her soft, sensuous form as he helped her up onto the lip of the pool. He hauled himself up and sat beside her, stroking her face gently. She was shivering, and it wasn't all about the cool of the night air, he could tell.

She snatched up the towel he offered her

from a nearby chaise lounge and dabbed at her makeup. Her eyes were now ringed like those of a raccoon, and her rouge and lipstick were smeared clownlike across her flesh. Maxwell took the towel from her, dabbed it in the pool, and helped wipe off the rest of her makeup.

"There, you don't need any of that," he told her honestly. "You're far more beautiful without it."

Her smile flickered faintly. "I'm such a klutz," she whispered. "I wanted this to be perfect. I wanted you to see me as your rescuer, your salvation. But all I do is fall into your arms like a schoolgirl with two left feet and a childish crush."

Maxwell's brow furrowed at this, his heart thundering. "What an odd thing to say," he muttered. "What the devil makes you think I need rescuing?"

"Hush," she said, her hand reaching for his. "We both know it's true."

He looked at her, seeing her for the first time as she truly was, and he knew that not only was she right, but that her sweet, kooky behavior masked an inner intensity, a fierce, determined spirit.

She sang:

From afar I have watched you, and seen
your secret dreams.
I can grant you all you wish for, impossible
though it seems.

*You will not age, you will not fade, your
legacy and your light,
Will be kept alive within these walls by
Emily's power and might.*

As she sang, lights exploded against the darkness, arcane energies swirled, and Maxwell felt light-headed. He drew away from the beautiful Emily, shaking, quaking, his flesh tingling as the lights struck through him and lifted him high.

He was floating! In fact, raising his hand before his face, he realized that he could see right through his own flesh. And another voice was calling to him. No, not a voice, more a force of will, the most powerful force he had ever felt.

Unable to resist, he allowed himself to be carried back on a magical wind toward the great house.

He never saw the witch's tear as the mansion swallowed him whole.

Gino burst from the house. He'd raced from his post the moment the fireworks had begun. "Mr. Maxwell, I—"

"There," the woman said, nodding toward the mansion.

Gino whirled around just in time to see the streaking, spiraling amber lights that now filled the space where Robert Maxwell had been a moment earlier. The actor appeared within that space for an instant, his gaze flickering in every direction before he nodded, smiled, and settled back. The lights shattered as they fell against the wall and vanished like fairy dust, leaving no trace of Robert Maxwell.

Gino turned back—but the woman was gone too. Out of breath, he clutched his knees and tried to make sense out of what he had heard and seen. *Emily. She called herself "Emily" in that rhyme she sang!*

Gino yelped as he felt someone tap him on the shoulder. He darted back—but no one was there.

"Well," said a ghostly voice. "Now ain't that a kick in the head?"

Twitching in terror, Gino bolted in the opposite direction, trying to convince himself that the voice he'd just heard did not belong to his employer.

The ghostly presence chased him until he was outside the grounds. Gino heard the gates rattle behind him, then felt the spirit presence slipping away, the chill lifting, the strange tingling along the hairs of his arms and neck settling down at last. Whatever it was, it could not follow him beyond the mansion's grounds.

Gino relaxed his grip on the door of his car and, despite his better judgment, looked back to the gates through which he had only just escaped.

Escaped? What a strange way to think of it.

He had served faithfully in this house for years, it was his entire life. What had he been thinking, running from it like a madman or a fool, he—then he saw it.

An amorphous figure pressed up near the open space between the gates, unwilling—or unable—to take another step closer. Gino squinted, not quite sure what he was looking at. The form before him shimmered and changed, one moment looking like a swashbuckler from a bygone age; the next a hulking, hooded executioner bearing a gleaming ax; the next a laughing vaudevillian in a pin-striped suit hefting a cherry pie.

"Mr. Maxwell?" Gino said. He edged forward a few inches, then whipped back as he felt the chill once more, the feeling of an absence, a strange void in reality where the unearthly figure stood.

Then the figure retreated and the chill eased. "Good-bye, my friend," said the ghostly voice. "Be seeing you."

"Not if I see you first," Gino said in a pained whisper.

Laughter drifted from the house as Gino made for his car and sped away into the night.

Chapter 1

San Francisco, Present Day

The Moon Festival was in full swing as the Charmed Ones wove their way through the swelling, bustling crowd that filled Chinatown for the occasion. Wild strips of cloth whipped at the darkened starry sky as, there upon the Washington Street main stage, dancers performed an elaborate and beautiful ceremony with ten-foot-long black, green, and crimson silk ribbons.

Phoebe spun at the sound of a great collective gasp and applauded as some participants carried a great dragon through the narrow, winding streets while others held fiery lanterns high to light their way. The festival was breathtaking!

"Come on, we don't get over here nearly enough," Phoebe said. "Can we stop in at the Golden Gate Fortune Cookie Company? Can we, can we, *please*?"

Piper shook her head shrewdly at Phoebe's silly, childlike chant. "Too bad we're here for work, not pleasure."

"Who says it can't be both?" Phoebe commented, slightly smacking her sister's arm with her elbow and nodding toward a couple of cute Asian men on the corner. "I mean, look at that great-lookin' guy givin' you the eye. Besides, how can you call it work? We don't get paid for saving Innocents. And the first rule is that magic is never to be used for personal gain, and—"

"You know what I meant," Piper told her.

"Sure I do," Phoebe said with a laugh. "I just like seeing those little crinkles at the corners of your eyes when you make your crabby squinty face."

"I do not have crinkles!" Piper objected. "And I do not have a crabby squinty face either, whatever that is."

Phoebe smiled, her pleasing banter an attempt to deal with the strong empathic vibe she'd picked up from all the immigrants who lived in this part of town for over a century. She could understand why a demon would be drawn to this area, so drenched in history and conflict, so alive with the crowds of people who had left their stamp on the very air that she was breathing. She looked to her strangely silent half-sister Paige.

Alongside her sisters, Paige passed a table fully loaded with smiling plastic Buddhas and nearly collided with a woman chowing down on bok choy, who sneered at her with annoyance. Paige darted back, apologizing, and was careful not to trip over the elaborate crepe paper dragons that lined the cobblestone streets.

Phoebe patted Paige's arm. "You seem a million miles away."

Paige shrugged. "Got a date. Gonna be late."

"That Kevin guy?" asked Phoebe. "Mister Hotshot Hollywood?"

Laughing despite herself, Paige allowed her loving sister to lift her from her glum mood. "Yeah. He's in town doing some location scouting for a personal project."

Phoebe nodded. "He's what, a director?"

"Writer, for now," she said. "But he just sold a screenplay for a mean bundle and he's meeting with investors to fund one he wants to direct."

"Wow," Phoebe said. "And you knew him when, huh?"

"We've been friends a long time," Paige admitted. Then, with a delighted sigh, she added, "And more than friends for a stretch. . . ."

Piper slid between her siblings. "Earth to Charmed Ones. If you can recall, we're here because we got a tip off from a very *highly placed source*, that the demon that's been causing us a boatload of grief for the last week was going to strike here tonight. Let's stay focused here, people."

"Better yet," hissed an icy voice from a slanting rooftop at their backs, "don't, and let us have our fun!"

Fiery lanterns flew at the Charmed Ones.

Piper's hands quickly shot up and blew a half dozen of the blinding, streaking lanterns into bits while Phoebe spun high and smacked three away with her high kicks and Paige orbed two more out of sight. The trio pressed together, back to back, surveying the crowd, which had barely registered the craziness amidst their celebrating.

"I'd say the whole battle thing's started up," Phoebe whispered breathlessly. "What do you think?"

"I think tonight's big bad was expecting us and set a trap," Paige hissed. "Just remember, this is a demon of illusions. Whatever he throws at us, it just isn't real!"

Piper surveyed the rooftops and pointed at a collection of dark, darting shapes above. "We've got to get the fighting away from all these Innocents. Up there!"

Phoebe and Paige followed their sister's gaze and spotted a legion of black-clad warriors racing across the rooftop.

Paige grabbed her sisters' hands and orbed them up to the roof, where warriors were ready and waiting. Moving with practiced grace, the Charmed Ones spread out to better deal with their enemies.

"Can't we just grab a nice cup of tea and talk this over, guys?" asked Piper nicely.

Several of the fighters raised spears tipped with sharp, curved blades.

"I'll take that as a no," said Piper.

"I can handle this," stated Phoebe, confidently striding before her sisters. Her former husband, Cole, had been a master of demonic martial arts, and he had taught her well. "After all, they're just illusions, right? They can't really hurt me so long as I—"

A spinning shuriken, a multipointed, razor-sharp throwing star, soared through the air, streaking against the billowing sleeve of Phoebe's blouse and shredding it like rice paper. She gulped. "Piper . . . ?"

"Oh wait, this demon can give his illusions form and substance," Piper said. "We may have a harder time with this than I thought."

The fighters fanned out, revealing that they were three score more in number than they had first appeared; the group with the spears was only the first wave.

"Eek!" cried Phoebe as the fighters rushed forward and sharp spears stabbed at her from every direction. "Ladies! I could use some help."

"Really?" asked Piper. "You amaze me."

Piper and Paige stepped up and took on a handful of the men with swords and other exotic-looking weapons.

"Swords!" cried Paige. She nearly toppled as a double armful of swords materialized in her hands. Piper froze one battalion of warriors racing toward her, and blew up the next!

Paige found herself trapped between two surging lines of heavily armed warriors. She stared at them with open panic, waited until the last possible second, then orbed herself away from their midst, the familiar blue-white light of her half-Whitelighter power taking her to safety on the far edge of the roof. Behind her, the surprised groups of berserker warriors sliced, diced, and otherwise vanquished each other!

"A nice warmup," rumbled a low voice that echoed through the night while the festival went on in full swing. It was the demon they had come to fight, but it was remaining unseen . . . for now. "Let's see how you face a greater challenge."

With a sudden flash, all the warriors on the roof vanished, and a trio of raging, roaring Chinese dragons burst to life in the night sky. The crowd cheered, believing they were watching elaborate fireworks or special effects.

The first dragon was composed of fierce bursts of golden fire, and it seared the rooftops with its low, trembling breath. The second dragon was also of the elements, with its clear watery frame ebbing and flowing as it flew high and sailed over the witches' heads, appearing like glass or ice. The third was made of air, and as it flew above the Charmed Ones, it whipped the cool night air into a small whirlwind.

The whirlwind struck at the sisters, blowing them high into the air and dropping them onto three separate rooftops.

The dragon of air raced at Piper. She tried to

freeze it, but the dragon immediately dissipated into a million separate bursts of chill air that she could not target, then re-formed instantly to swoop down and swipe at her.

"Yikes!" she hollered, ducking its tearing, shredding claws. Piper tried to blow the dragon up, but it simply exploded into a thousand smaller whirlwinds, which came together an instant later to drive down at her.

On another rooftop, Phoebe was face-to-face with the dragon of water. Every punch and kick she delivered to the beast had no more effect than striking at a pool of water. The dragon's body flowed around her blows, absorbing the speed and thrust of her attacks. Then it solidified, its great maw and mighty claws striking and smacking her off her feet.

The most dangerous dragon of all set after Paige upon the final rooftop: the dragon of fire. Paige orbed from the path of its fiery attacks, watching with horror as wide swaths of rooftop burst into sizzling flame. No matter where she rematerialized, the dragon was right there, ready to attack again. Each time, she missed its fatal, fetid, fiery breath by a matter of seconds—and centimeters.

Paige looked over to see the dragons of water and air drowning and suffocating her sisters. She had time for only one bold move, and so she orbed in next to Phoebe. Paige's golden flaming pal followed her, and burst into existence in the

exact same spot as its watery brother. The
dragon of air saw what was about to happen
and raced to its brethren, but it arrived in time
only to share their fate rather than pull them
apart. The fire and water turned to steam, which
in turn struck at and diffused the dragon of air.

Phoebe collapsed to the ground, gasping for
air. Paige bent down to make sure her sister was
okay as Piper bounded to their rooftop. The sisters were soaked and covered in soggy soot,
their outfits ruined. Fortunately, Paige had left
her dinner dress in the car, where she would
pick it up before orbing to the restaurant.

Suddenly, a heavy wind kicked up around
them and a demon of illusions appeared, the
moon wreathing his impressive form. In appear-
ance, it was one of the most classically styled
demons the Charmed Ones had ever beheld.
Huge, curling horns drove its height beyond ten
feet, its leering, sharp-featured face ended in a
forked goatee while its wild ebony hair whipped
about the rippling muscles of its overdeveloped
frame. Gleaming spikes and black, curling tat-
toos adorned the demon's otherwise bare chest,
and its legs tapered into goatlike limbs and
hooves. Naturally, talonlike nails tipped the
demon's long fingers. Only its flesh was any sort
of revelation, a bold emerald rather than the
fiery red of the Underworld.

"Diggin' the retro look," Paige said. "Classic
evil never goes out of style, right?"

The demon hissed and flexed his talons, his eyes blazing with murderous light.

"Now, what is it you're called again?" asked Piper. "Your demon clan name, I mean? Oh, wait, that's right, I remember now. Thirdus from the Leftus, right? The guys that always get vanquished first?"

"I am M'Gohrathet of the Clan Eesleviathan!" the demon roared. "My kind has wormed its way into the nightmares and legends of humanity since its very beginnings. Tonight, I will draw these human fools' belief in their made-up deities as fuel for my illusionary legions, making them real so that I might conquer the world of men and—"

"Yeah, yeah, yadda, yadda, look at me, I'm big and bad, Daddy didn't love me," Piper said with a sigh. "Come on, is that *really* what you want us to put on your tombstone?"

"I will take the power of these people's illusions," he repeated, "and I will—"

"Yeah, well, little problem there," Phoebe pointed out. "Met their gods already. They're real."

The demon spit and snarled, "They are not!"

"Are too, are too!" Paige taunted. "Think about it, buddy. Who do you think tipped us off that you were going to be here acting all nefarious and whatever tonight?"

"That means you don't have *squat* to draw on for power," Phoebe said. "Sorry, Charley!"

The demon shuddered. "You lie! And you mock me at your own peril. I need only wave my hand and all three of you will be *doomed*!"

"Aw, sheez, doomed again?" quipped Piper. "Well, then it must be Thursday. Thursdays are our usual day for being doomed. Friday is facing Ultimate Trials and Unthinkable Torments, and Saturday is for the Peril so Great, We Must Not Speak Its Name."

Phoebe nodded. "Oh, right, that one. Laundry day."

Howling in fury, the demon waved his hand and darksome forms took shape around the Charmed Ones. Even without the power of the festival goers to draw upon, the demon had plenty of juice!

"Do you know the legend of the Moon Festival?" boomed the terrifying demon. "A person would sit under the full moon knowing that their loved one, even though they were not together, was sitting under that same full moon thousands of miles away eating the same kind of moon cake so it seemed they were together for that blissful moment."

"So you're here to eat a moon pie with your girlfriend?" queried Phoebe.

"That's so corny," stated Piper.

"No!" shrieked the demon. "I simply wanted you to know your fate. Tonight, I make my moon cake from your bones!"

The demon lunged at the sisters, his eyes filling with flames. The sisters found themselves surrounded by a man-size shadow with raking talons.

"Okay," Piper said. "We conned him into showing himself. I think now's a good time to finish this doofus off!"

Phoebe tossed a potion at the demon, stopping it in its tracks. The shadow forms it had summoned disappeared back into the darkness as the Charmed Ones chanted:

> *Demon of this, Demon of that,*
> *Keep your illusions under your hat,*
> *You've been a pest, but we're the best,*
> *So we vanquish thee with all the rest!*

Arcane fires leaped up at the demon's cloven feet and soared around it. It stood still, trembling with agony but grinning nonetheless. "Enjoy the time remaining to you witches. . . . I will be avenged!"

Smiling grimly, the demon vanished in a fiery torrent.

Phoebe frowned as she watched the last remnants of the demon disappear into the night. On the streets below, the festival was still in full swing and the Innocents were safe.

Piper eyed her sister with interest. "Okay, I'll bite. What's bugging you?"

"Just . . ." Phoebe shrugged. "I don't know, I've heard a lot of demons swear all kinds of things when they're being vanquished. . . ."

"Really?" asked Paige, wishing she had a
blow-dryer for her hair. "I thought most of them
just yelped a lot."

Piper raised a quiet finger and held it out
menacingly. "Hush. Yeah, so?"

"This one sounded like he really meant it,"
Phoebe said, hugging herself as the cool night
air washed over her and she shivered. "He
didn't even scream when he went up in flames
either. He just looked at us. It was eerie. What if
there really is something to it?"

Piper rolled her eyes. "Then we'll deal, like
we always do. Isn't there somewhere you need
to be?"

With a laugh, Paige said, "You know it,
sister!"

Paige orbed herself and her sisters back to
their car, where she picked up her dress. "I think
I'll have to hit the Manor real fast to fix my hair
and makeup. You girls want a lift so you can
clean up quicker? Leo could orb you back here
to pick up the car. . . ."

"Nah, that's okay," Phoebe said, kissing Paige
on the cheek. "You go have fun!"

The happy, auburn-haired witch orbed away
into the night.

Paige Matthews didn't see the strange shadowy figure that had been watching her and her
fellow Charmed Ones for the last few minutes,
eyes blazing with hatred.

Chapter 2

Paige arrived at the elegant—and packed—Italian restaurant a full thirty minutes late. The lovely amber glow of candlelight rose from the main dining hall, striking sparks against fluted wineglasses, crystal chandeliers, and intricately designed golden picture frames that bore museum-caliber Renaissance-era portraits of the old country. Faces from the society pages laughed, smiled, and celebrated the good life as they devoured swordfish steaks or elaborate pasta dishes straight from Tuscany.

She immediately caught sight of Kevin and covered her face with her hands in mock shame, playfully peering at him between crisscrossed fingers as he rose from their table and motioned to her. Snagging a menu, she pantomimed taking a big honkin' bite from it in frustration, then tossed it back to the reservations desk, rolled her eyes, threw up her hands, and mouthed, *"I'm so sorry."* Dipping her head low, she scurried across the tasteful but passionate burgundy carpet toward him.

Kevin looked gorgeous, of course. His tall, bronzed, muscular form, honed during his early teenage years in Australia, had been poured into a fitted pair of black slacks, a black silk short-sleeve shirt, and a matching black vest. He adjusted his slim and sleek pure white tie, his biceps and forearm muscles coiling as he moved to get her chair. Not that she was noticing his better-than-ever physique, or anything.

Not that much, anyway.

Paige slinked into her chair, showing off her own off-the-shoulder elegant black evening dress and shawl, a stunning crisscross lattice-work descending from her collarbone and streaking toward her low-cut bodice. Laughing, she rolled her eyes. "I'm so sorry I'm late. Last-second family emergency, you know how it is."

"It's fine," Kevin assured her. "Is everything okay?"

She raised an eyebrow in confusion.

"Family emergency," he prompted, scratching the side of his head lightly, his fingers neatly treading his bright blond highlights. The man could easily have been an actor.

"Oh, oh—that!" She laughed. "Family thinks everything's an emergency, don'tcha know! I'm just sorry you've been here waiting all by yourself."

"Hasn't been so bad," Kevin said, angling his

head to an almost imperceptible degree toward the bar. There, a lovely, raven-haired woman who must have spent half the night wriggling into her little black dress looked over her shoulder at Kevin, eyeing him with open interest despite Paige's presence.

Down, sister, Paige thought. *I saw him first!*

He laughed. "Don't worry, she's not really my type. As you know."

With a catlike grin, Paige settled back in her chair. "Oh? So what is your type these days?" She absently twisted her own auburn locks and raised an eyebrow. "Still have a thing for redheads?"

Their waiter arrived an instant before Kevin might reply. Instead, the handsome wonder-from-down-under nodded toward the menu that had drifted smoothly into Paige's grasp and said, "Chef Nunzio makes an excellent lobster and shrimp fra diavolo. Just the right amount of parsley and ground red pepper."

"I'll have that," she said, her gaze riveted to his stunning eyes.

He ordered minestrone soup and their entrées, and told the waiter to take his time, they were in no hurry. A large bottle of champagne lazily lay in a bucket of ice between Paige and her . . . date? Was this a date? Kevin was an old flame whom she hadn't seen in ages, yet this certainly felt like a date.

"I should have asked if you were hungry,"

Kevin said apologetically. "If you've already eaten, I can just get the waiter back and we could skip right to dessert."

Paige smiled. *Dessert? Only if you're on the menu, hot stuff!*

"Are you kidding?" she said, extending her toes and lightly brushing Kevin's leg under the table. "I'm starving!"

Kevin drew in a sharp, excited breath, but otherwise acted as if he hadn't noticed Paige's tiny bout of toe frolics. Easing her foot back, Paige hid her smile behind her steepled fingers. *Bad witch, bad!* She chided herself. *Keep the tootsie to yourself . . . at least until dinner arrives.* But she kept on smiling.

They chitchatted, opened the champagne, toasted each other's successes, and settled into a fizzy bubbly place of contentment that had everything to do with the comfortable loving connection they shared as old friends and lovers.

Paige studied Kevin and realized that, honestly, she could not have cared less that he was now rich and successful, except that the validations of his worth as a storyteller had filled him with a visible confidence. As they played catch-up, he bounced and bounded in his chair, his hands wildly doing the talking for him. His eyes didn't just twinkle, they flared like twin supernovas, and his smile was wide enough and bright enough to light up the heavens.

Paige's lips quirked in a goofy grin as she

raised an eyebrow. "This isn't just about your big movie deal, is it?" She slapped her knee and said, in a mock Midwestern farm-girl accent, "Well, if I didn't know better, I'd be thinkin' this'n is plum darn in luvvv!"

He blushed—no, not just blushed, he *flushed*.

"All right, hoss, I've got you now," she whispered, dropping the fake accent, her drawl transforming into a steamy sigh of delectable delights. The accent had come from a play he had written when they were in school together that she had often helped him rehearse. "So who's the lucky girl?"

He squinted—and squirmed. But happily.

He wouldn't look her way either, he just kept smiling happily as if he was about to reveal a carefully guarded secret that he'd been dying to tell for who knows how long.

Paige watched as his bouncing became fidgeting and she thought, *Wow, this is like that time in the 10th grade when he was trying to get up the courage to ask me to the big dance and—*

Oh, my gosh! It's me. I'm the one he's head over heels in love with!

Paige suddenly heard Phoebe's voice in her head, Phoebe speaking in her most piercing, therapist-like way, *And how do you feel about that?* As if in answer, Paige's toes curled, and she felt a happy little flush her own self. She leaned forward just a little and let her low-cut dress communicate volumes.

Strangely, Kevin didn't seem to notice.

"Who *is* the lucky girl?" asked Paige with a slight edge, suspicion that she wasn't the object of his desire creeping into her tone.

"You remember Cassie?" he asked.

Paige's eyes flashed open wide. "Cassie the Conqueror? How could I forget? First girl in our school to join the wrestling team. Not that she wasn't drop-dead gorgeous with a rockin' bod, but . . . what? You told her and you won't tell me?"

"Not exactly, uh—"

"No, wait! I remember now, that whole thing from two months ago that was in the newspapers. Cassie doing the real-life superhero thing. She works in a comic book shop now, right, and there was a fire across the street, that girl was trapped on the fourth floor. . . . The fire trucks hadn't gotten there yet and Cassie climbed up the fire escape, kicked in a window, and saved the kid. That was pretty awesome, I've gotta admit. And you wrote an article about it, didn't you? You even sent it to me. That was your last story for the magazine just before you sold your screenplay, right?"

"Yeah," he said dreamily. "I hadn't seen Cassie in a long time, and then she just walked back into my life and everything turned around, I sold my script—it almost all became perfect. The only thing that's not perfect about my life right now is—"

"That she's not in it," Paige said, finally catching on, her heart sinking, but only a little. "It's Cassie. You are so totally in love with her!"

"Always have been," he admitted.

She frowned. "You mean even when we—"

"No! You know what I mean." He reached across the table and took her hand. "I love you, Paige. Always have, always will. Five years ago we both needed to know if the connection we shared meant that we were supposed to be something more than best friends in the world. And being boyfriend and girlfriend was great for both of us, for a while. But in the end, it almost ruined everything else we had, and losing you forever like that would have been the saddest thing that could have ever happened to me."

Her own radiant smile returned. He was right! "You always did know just the right thing to say. So Cassie's the one, huh?"

"She is." A look of sadness eased into his eyes.

"But she doesn't know it," Paige said, filling in the silence.

"Well, that kind of brings us to this weekend," Kevin said. "I'm throwing a party. Cassie's going to be there. In fact, the party's in honor of all my friends who have given me so much over the years. Now I have a chance to start giving something back. I'm not going to miss that chance."

"Am I invited?" Paige asked.

"No, absolutely not," Kevin said quickly. "Of course! What do you think? It'll be a blast. I'm having the whole thing catered, there's a band, games, an events coordinator, it'll be awesome."

Paige was impressed. "Wow, what'd you do, rent a whole floor at some hotel?"

"Even better. The party's going to be at my house. In Hollywood. I want you to be there. I *need* you to be there. I never could have done any of this without you."

Paige winked. "Of *course* I'll come!"

"The thing is, I have another reason for asking you," Kevin admitted. "I need your help with Cassie."

"My help?" Paige asked, taking another sip of wine as their soup arrived. "You've never exactly been the shy type. What do you need me to do?"

Kevin was sweating. "This is it for me. I know it. I live or die by my instincts, Paige. You know that. I can feel it in my bones that this weekend is either the dealmaker or the dealbreaker for Cassie and me. I've got to go for it, to tell her how I feel, how I've always felt. It's just—"

"Oh, come on," Paige cried. "You're not going to try to make me believe that *you're* at a loss for words, are you?"

"When I'm around her? Sometimes, yeah. The right words." He looked at her with pleading eyes. "Will you help me?"

"Yes," Paige said. "Anything, always. You know that."

He smiled. "Same back atcha!"

Paige leaned back in her seat. "So, let's get back to . . . you bought a house? That's wonderful!"

"More than a house. A mansion."

"Whoa, Nellie!" Paige murmured in concern. "Don't you think you might be moving a little too fast? I mean, how much is the studio paying you, anyway?"

Grinning, Kevin slipped a pen from his vest and scribbled a number on a napkin. He passed it to Paige—and she blanched.

Nodding at a number she wasn't sure she would ever earn in her entire life, Paige said, "Mansion's a good, nice solid investment, something to do with your leftover lunch money. . . ."

He laughed. "It's not really as extravagant as it sounds. The place was a steal."

"Really?" Paige asked. She found that hard to believe. "We're talking an actual Hollywood mansion, where movie stars used to live."

"One in particular. Ever hear of Robert Maxwell?"

She cocked an eyebrow. "Sounds *vaguely* familiar."

"Don't let him hear you say that."

"Exsqueeze me?"

Kevin spread his hands wide. "He was the biggest star in Hollywood, once upon a time.

Nineteen-twenty-six, as a matter-of-fact. The year he mysteriously disappeared."

"Hang on. Dial it back to this guy hearing things."

His smile couldn't have gone any wider. "That's why the place was such a steal. The mansion's haunted by Maxwell's spirit!"

Back at the Halliwell Mansion, Paige plopped backward down into the couch, her feet sticking up in the air, her shoes dangling. She had just finished relating the story about the haunted house her pal Kevin had purchased, and she couldn't stop giggling over it. Phoebe drifted over and tickled Paige's bare soles, transforming her giggles into squealing peels of laughter.

"Whoa, since when is a haunting funny and cool?" asked Piper. A baby monitor sat beside her, its on button pressed, even though Leo was upstairs with Wyatt. She occasionally heard a baby rattle, or the sound of Leo giving the baby yet another airplane ride!

On the couch, Paige narrowly escaped another surging attack of Phoebe the tickle-monster and blew the bangs from before her face. "I don't think the place is *really* haunted. I've just got the giggles remembering some of the stories Kevin told me about the Hollywood types he's dealing with now." She nodded to Phoebe. "You thought all of Cole's plans to become the new Source and take over were wacky; you should hear what these guys do to one another to get a corner office!"

Paige settled back into the couch, her smile quickly fading.

"So why the worry face?" asked Piper.

"I do *not* have a worry face," Paige declared, pressing her lips together in a mock-serious expression.

Piper frowned. "If I have a crabby squinty face with crinkles, you have a worry face."

"Okay, I'm a little worried," Paige admitted. "Kevin's my friend. I don't want anything happening to him."

Phoebe smacked her hands together. "Time to turn to my trusty laptop and see what I can dig up on this Robert Maxwell guy and his home sweet home. . . ."

Piper watched from the love seat as Phoebe sank into the couch next to Paige and booted up her machine.

"Really not worried," Paige assured Piper.

"I hear ya," Piper said. "But do I believe ya? That's the question!"

"Pretty straightforward haunting stuff," Phoebe said, pouring over a site devoted entirely to the Maxwell house. "Lots of crazy, creepy poltergeist action—y'know: levitating furniture whipping around in a whirlwind, ghouls and ghosties and long-legged beasties, all that."

Paige sat up sharply. "Anyone ever get hurt?

Any disappearances or—y'know, demises?"

Phoebe's gaze narrowed. "Actually, no—not so far as I can tell, not once in all these years since Maxwell disappeared. Lots of folks tried sneaking into the house and got scared off, but no one was ever hurt—which is kinda strange with a haunting, if you really think about it. In fact, here's an account of a contractor who was brought in to do some remodeling about ten years ago, and he says the ghost saved his life!"

"Huh!" Piper said, sipping at a cup of green tea that had been cooling beside her. "Different."

Phoebe comfortably nestled in the couch so she could tell the story. "Says here it was the middle of the night. He had stayed to finish some plans that he had to present in the morning when all the ghostly stuff kicked in. All of a sudden, this guy riding a black horse came charging at him out of nowhere, a headless dude wearing period clothing. But he carried a big fiery carved pumpkin head and just as the contractor stumbled out of the house, the rider threw the pumpkin right at him. He screamed and ran in a blind panic, not seeing the nice big empty Olympic-size pool right in his way. He ran right over the edge, looked down, and saw the drop underneath him. His legs were kicking, his arms pinwheeling, but he didn't fall. Something had a hold of him by the back of his shirt collar. Whatever it was gently hauled him to safety and dropped him down into a chaise lounge, where a margarita appeared. The contractor heard a voice say, 'Sorry about that, friend, sometimes I get a little carried away.' When the contractor whirled around in the direction of the voice, there was nothing to see."

Paige frowned in confusion. "But Kevin said it was Maxwell who haunted the place. . . ."

"I'm getting to that," Phoebe assured her. "This guy, the contractor, abandoned the project, and nobody else was willing to touch it. But that voice stayed with him for years. Then, finally, he found a website devoted to Maxwell and heard a really old recording of the actor's voice. And what do you know? They were one and the same! And a margarita was the actor's favorite drink too."

"I'm guessing there were others who identified Maxwell?" asked Piper.

Phoebe nodded. "A few recognized him from old photos."

"Has anyone ever lived in the house since Maxwell disappeared?" Paige asked intently.

"Not for long," Phoebe replied. "The record is three weeks."

"Nice!" Piper said, putting down her tea. "Great place for a shindig. Let's hope none of the guests have weak hearts."

"So not funny," Paige said gravely.

Phoebe smiled. "Remember, it says here that no one's ever been hurt in the place. The ghost—"

"Alleged ghost, counselor!" Paige said, jamming

a finger toward the ceiling. "The supernatural's not always to blame."

"Well, duh . . . ," Phoebe muttered. "Like I was saying, the ghost, or whatever it is, just seems kinda, um, playful."

Piper began to pace. "But it scares people off."

"Yeah," Phoebe said, scrolling through another web page. "Or something does. But it doesn't hurt them."

"There's a first time for everything," Piper said. "I think we should all go. You never know when the Power of Three might be needed."

"And it should be one awesome party," Paige added. "Kevin's totally smokin', and I'd bet that most of his friends are too."

"Wow, sexy former flames," Piper teased, "that's your Kryptonite. I bet you still have the hots for this Kevin dude."

Paige rolled her eyes at the good-natured teasing. "I *told* you, he's totally in love with someone else."

"Like that's going to stop you," Piper muttered, resting her empty teacup in its saucer and settling back as she listened to Leo snoring on the baby monitor.

Paige sat up straight and pouted as she crossed her arms over her chest in mock hurt. "Hey! I'm a good girl."

Piper shrugged. "Yeah, except when you're not."

"You know what I mean," Paige said, taking the teasing good-naturedly. "I'll admit, my ego took a little beating at dinner, but I'm over it. Besides, if I still had a thing for him, do you really think I would invite you guys along to bust my chops?"

"It could be part of your bold and cunning plan," suggested Phoebe. "Tell you what, I'll make a bet with you. If you can get through the weekend without hooking up with this Kevin guy or one of his hottie pals, neither Piper nor I will ever tease you again about your love life. Whatcha say?"

With a grin, Paige nodded sharply and said, "I'll take that bet!"

Chapter 3

Sunlight burst from between dense leafy branches overhead as Piper's car wound along a twisting road guarded by ancient trees. The oaks leaned across the dirty road, their branches entwining high above as tiny, scurrying squirrels peered down and dropped acorns like guided missiles.

"They're doing it on purpose!" railed Piper as she gripped the wheel, her rooftop *thunk*ing and *plunk*ing as more acorns fell.

"Yes," Paige agreed. "It's a conspiracy. The forces of nature are letting us know, through their tiny little warrior avatars, that it's not safe up at Maxwell Manor, we must turn back, turn back, before it's too late!"

Phoebe smirked. "Nice one."

Piper ignored her and vented some more as she shook a fist high. "Stupid squirrels doing stupid squirrelly things. Ah, nuts . . ."

Paige and Phoebe broke into laughter as the car hurtled past the grove and a lovely shimmering lake appeared to their right.

"Ooh, ohh, this is it!" Paige said excitedly. "Take the first right after the lake—we're nearly there!"

Piper relaxed as they left the land of the savage squirrels.

The mansion, constructed of handmade red brick laid in the English bond style, was accented by sandstone quoins and window surrounds. A slate shingle roof flowed over the steeply pitched gable roof, sheltering more than 85,000 square feet of living space inside—a total of seventy-five rooms, including twenty-two bedrooms and fourteen bathrooms.

A four-story square tower capped with battlements and chimney flues guarded the main entry. Within the tower rose the grand stairway, illuminated by delicate stained-glass windows. Turrets and gables and countless windows watched the newcomers arrive like a host of silently watching eyes.

"Creepy much?" asked Piper. "Nah!" She whirled on her sisters. "Okay, the squirrels had the right idea. Let's turn back."

Paige rolled her eyes and laughed as Kevin appeared in the doorway to greet them. She ran to him and he gathered her up in his powerful arms, hugging her tight and swinging her around as she kicked her heels high in the air behind her.

He let her down as Phoebe and Piper caught up.

"Should we bring our luggage in and be shown to our rooms, good sir?" Paige asked with a bright smile. She spoke as if she were a fine lady in the olden times of England.

Kevin smiled warmly, exactly as a gallant knight should. "Not unless you want to change and freshen up first. I know you had a long drive. The rest of the guests are here, and this would be a good time for a guided tour."

"Sounds good to me!" Phoebe said. "I love big old mansions!"

He showed them into the vast, elegantly appointed receiving hall. A portrait of the handsome Robert Maxwell hung over the mantel, and several movie posters from the actor's film career lined the hall. The stained-glass windows all bore the marks of acting and stageplay: the masks of Comedy and Tragedy, a piece of parchment and a quill, hands pressed together in wild applause. Several suits of armor lined the hall, standing sentinel before life-size paintings of the mansion's previous actor-owners decked out in their greatest roles. Macbeth, Hamlet, Henry V were just some of the characters boldly peering at passersby.

A modern elevator and a private telephone room were hidden behind panels in the first-floor Linenfold Hallway, named for its custom-designed linenfold wood paneling, handcarved to resemble delicate folds of fabric. In other parts of the mansion, oak, sandalwood, and black walnut paneling covered the walls.

Kevin eased himself before Phoebe and said, "I've read your column."

Phoebe's eyes lit up. "You have?"

He nodded and awarded her with his most dazzling smile. "Absolutely terrific stuff. You've got a very unique voice and style, and you help a lot of people. I'm a big fan."

"Well," Phoebe said, grinning wildly and spinning toward Paige to mouth the words, *"Where have you been keeping this one?"*

Paige rolled her eyes. And her sisters called *her* man-crazy!

Kevin looked to Piper and took her hand. "Piper, this is a real honor. I have a question: P3 is awesome, just love it—"

"You've been there?" asked Paige.

"A couple of times, yeah, before you found your sisters," Kevin explained.

Piper nodded. "You should stop in now. We've made a bunch of changes."

"I will," Kevin promised. "My question is this: Do you think you'll ever go back to your haute cuisine roots? Because, as a chef, you were unrivaled. I used to save up to eat at restaurants where you were running the kitchen."

"Okeydokey," Piper said, narrowing her gaze playfully while loving the adoration. "If you were going to butter me up any more, you'd have to serve me as French bread."

But Kevin meant every word he said, and all three of the sisters could see that. His sincerity radiated from his perfect emerald eyes. "Before we worry about that tour, I was wondering if I could have a moment alone with the lovely Paige?"

"Sure!" Piper said. "We'll just wander a bit, give you two a chance to catch up."

"Rrrrrrraow!" Phoebe added, making a cat-clawed scratch in the air as she winked and caught up to Piper, who was already and adroitly making herself scarce.

"What was that?" asked Kevin, repeating Phoebe's catlike motion.

Paige wasn't about to explain that her sisters thought she was so man-crazy that she would find some way to hook up with Kevin despite everything she'd told them. "Love 'em to pieces, but my sisters are nuts, don't mind them. So what's up?"

Kevin let out a long ragged breath as his calm demeanor vanished. "Cassie's here and I'm losing it. I don't think I've ever been this nervous in my entire life. I haven't been able to say two words to her. Well, maybe two words. 'Hi' and 'here.' But that's all I've managed."

Paige smiled. "Okay, just remember, deep breaths. In through the nose, out through the mouth."

"She brought this guy with her," Kevin said, scratching the side of his head just over his left ear. "I think he's an investor."

"That's good!" Paige said happily. "She's taking an interest in helping you launch your career as a director. Awesome! You know, it sounds to me like you really don't need a lot of help from yours truly."

Suddenly, a stunning pixieish beauty breezed by. She had model-perfect French-*Vogue* features; wide, dark wondrous eyes; and wild rainbow streaks of color in her dark pageboy do. Her tight black skull-and-crossbones ripped tank top revealed well-tanned and perfectly honed shoulders, arms, and abs, and her low-riding jeans spilled into bright emerald faux-alligator boots. Her figure was, by anyone's standards, to die for.

And she was so tiny!

Cassie swooped and swerved, a darling dervish of unbelievable energy, deftly diving between the pair on her way to another room. "Oh! 'Scuse me." She flashed her dazzling smile at Paige without stopping. "Hi!"

With that, Cassie was gone, but her presence had had an effect. Paige's gaze whipped back to Kevin. His face was flushed red, a thin sheen of cold sweat covered him, he was trembling, his throat making dry gasping sounds, eyes wide enough to pop.

"Okay," she said, steering him to the hidden room behind the paneling. It was dark and dank—and very private. From here, she had a view of the unbelievably large and elaborate dining hall where the other guests mingled. "I take that back. You need all the help you can get!"

Paige peeked into the dining hall while Kevin handled his hyperventilating and surveyed the party. People were serving themselves from a long buffet table, and a hot-looking, dark-haired guy in an apron was clearly doing kitchen duty.

"What's missing from this picture?" she wondered aloud.

The stage was empty, the unattended drum kit catching the light and reflecting it back like an eager pet wanting to be played with while keyboards collected dust and guitars and other instruments rested forlornly on their stands.

"So what happened to the band?" asked Paige.

Kevin shrugged. "Well, there was a thing that happened this afternoon, before anyone else showed up."

"What kind of thing?" Paige asked.

He looked away, smiling sheepishly. "It's nothing. . . ."

Paige wasn't about to be put off so easily. "Come on, give. What happened?"

"Well, the band was in here practicing, running a short set, and they had their crew, their electricians and carpenters and everyone getting the place up to specs so they could really put on a bangin' show, when, um . . . look, it's crazy."

"Kevin, details."

He sighed. "They all started singing opera.

Couldn't stop. Operettas at the top of their lungs until their throats were raw. It kept going until they were off the grounds. Every one of them said it was because they were hearing opera music and it was so deafening, the only way they could cope was to sing along."

Paige shook her head. "That's one way to break a contract and go do another gig, I suppose. At least none of them said they saw some wacky-looking guy in a black cloak and hat wearing a white mask over half his face."

Kevin gulped.

"Kidding," Paige explained. "Phantom of the Opera? Just a joke, or, wait, did someone—"

"Two of them saw the Phantom," Kevin admitted. "One said the phantom goosed him!"

Paige drew back and crossed her arms over her chest. "Now I know you're making this up."

Kevin sighed. "I wish . . ."

"And not that I'm complaining—what girl doesn't like the personal attention—but I thought you said you had an events coordinator coming in, and staff, and all that? Why are your pals serving everything?"

Kevin scratched his stubble. "A few more things happened when they showed up."

"Okay . . . hit me."

"There was a food fight," Kevin said. "Except—no one was throwing the food. It was tossing itself all over the place. It made a heck of a mess."

Paige's brow furrowed as she scrutinized the dining hall. It looked spotless now. "So the caterers and everyone ran screaming, covered in mayo and eggs and salad dressing and who knows what, and then they came back to clean up the place for you?"

"Well . . . no." He scratched the side of his head, well aware of how crazy all of this was sounding. "They were just . . . one minute they were moving furniture around, and there was this big table they wanted to get out of the way, the one with the gargoyle claws on the feet? But there was no way. The table just wouldn't fit through the doors. The only thing that made any sense about how the table got there in the first place is that the doors must have been wider at one time, then it got divided up after that table had been moved in. So they wanted to saw it in half and move it to one of the guesthouses. They said they'd put it back together later, after they got it down to size. And, uh, that's about when the food started flying."

"You didn't answer my question," Paige reminded him. "How'd the place get so neat and tidy again? Did your pals help you clean it up? Did you do it by yourself?"

Kevin crossed his arms over his chest. "The truth? I don't know. I followed everyone outside and left a complete mess behind. When I came back a couple of minutes later, it had all been tidied up. Not a trace of all the gunk and goo was left. I don't know how it happened."

"Huh," said Paige. She knew that every haunted house carried a charge of some kind. They were like batteries with huge stores or reserves of psychic power. Was that the case with Maxwell Manor? Had Kevin just experienced poltergeist phenomena due to a leftover charge? Wondering how he viewed all this, she added, "And this strikes you as . . ."

He turned his thousand-watt smile on her. "Kinda cool, actually. Whoever, whatever, was behind this definitely has style!"

The hot guy in the wacky apron swung back out of the dining room and caught the couple as they were just about to join the party. Kevin grabbed him and introduced him as his pal Craig.

Craig was a walking cartoon, but in a good way—a six foot three, square-jawed hunk with jet-black hair that could only be described as aerodynamic. He had been a class clown all his life, using himself as the butt of his good-natured humor, and he had his own comedy club in the Valley. Bright red lobsters clutching doll-size humans in their claws overran his apron. The words, "At last, revenge!" swam above the silly image.

"Kev, buddy, you really outdid yourself with this place," Craig said. "I keep expecting Morticia Addams to step out of the kitchen and offer me some toadstool punch."

"And if she did?" asked Kevin.

"You know me. I'd get her number, brother. She's hot!" Craig peered at Paige. "And speaking of hot, why have I never met this friend of yours?"

Paige grinned. "Well hello to you, too."

Craig admiringly surveyed the manor. "Seriously, Kev, this place is beautiful, just perfect for you. Not that you need inspiration with that imagination of yours, but if you did, all you'd have to do is look around. I bet this place has some great stories to tell."

Another guest waved to Craig, and he quickly excused himself.

"So, does everyone know the place is supposed to be haunted?" asked Paige as she drew Kevin deeper down the hall.

Kevin nodded. "Everyone I invited here for the weekend? Yeah, absolutely. Why?"

"No reason . . ." Paige certainly hadn't ruled out the notion of an actual haunting, but it had just occurred to her that Kevin's pals might have all joined forces to have some fun with him this weekend and make the mansion appear haunted. She'd seen stranger things happen.

"All right, I just have one question about all this stuff you were describing, and I need you to be totally honest with me, you know I'd never judge you," Paige went on. "Ready?"

"Sure."

"Do *you* think the house is haunted?"

"No," Kevin said ruefully. "The truth is that no matter how much I might want to believe, I really don't. If I'm going to accept ghosts as a real possibility, I might as well start examining every woman I meet for strange birthmarks and assume that every soulless producer I meet in Hollywood either really did sell his soul to get where they are. Or has a battery of wizards working for him—as well as attorneys."

"Then how do you explain what's been happening here today?"

Kevin shrugged. "I don't know. I can't, not yet. Come on, we've probably kept your sisters waiting long enough."

Meanwhile, Piper and Phoebe had already met some of the guests. They stood before one of them now: a tall, frosty-eyed thin guy whose brown hair streaked to his eyebrows. He wore a T-shirt that read, "Does not play well with others (others have problem with losing)."

"I'm Karl," he said, sounding pained and bored.

"Oh, hey Karl," Phoebe said in her most chipper tone. "And what do you do?"

"I work in graphic animation."

Phoebe's interest was snagged. "Oh, like cartoons? That's awesome. I love that one with the talking squirrel. Did you do that?"

Karl's upper lip curled and quivered, and he shuddered at the affront. "No. Nothing like *that*. My company produces sophisticated web animations for Fortune 500 companies. We deal with high-level corporate branding. Important work, not trivialities."

"Huh!" Piper put in, disliking his demeanor already. "No talking squirrels, then."

"No," Karl said icily. "Excuse me. An empty glass makes for an unhappy Karl, and we can't have that." Karl snaked away toward the sprawling bar.

"Wow," Phoebe said. "Does he often talk about himself in the third person like that?"

"He does," Craig said as he swung near, offered hors d'oeuvres on a shiny silver plate, and swung away again.

The sisters saw Kevin and Paige ease into the enormous dining room, which boasted a trio of signed Tiffany chandeliers, centerpieces, and three equally long extraordinarily appointed dining tables large enough to feed Arthur, his knights, and all their cohorts. Kevin took the stage where the band's equipment still resided and raised his hand high.

"Okay, if I could have everyone's attention just for a moment," Kevin called, his voice cutting through the tide of laughter around him. "Please join me in welcoming our final three guests for the weekend, the Halliwell sisters Phoebe and Piper, and their half sister and my old dear friend Paige Matthews!"

The other party guests applauded and the Charmed Ones, now joined by Paige, all waved.

"A few changes to the agenda . . . ," Kevin went on. "I'm sure you're all wondering where the kitchen staff, servers, and the band, for that matter, have all gone. I'm afraid the ghost is to blame, or so it would appear. I'd say that the powers of darkness swallowed all of the help whole, but that would be an exaggeration. They just got a bad case of the willies and ran screaming, each and every one of them."

Craig laughed and rewarded his old friend with a dismissive wave of his hand. "Just tell 'em the truth: that you already went through all your money and weren't going to be able to pay 'em! No, wait. That was *me* who went through all your cash. I'm sorry!"

Everyone laughed.

Kevin went on: "I made calls to all their agencies about having replacements sent, but until that happens we're on our own."

"Hrmmph!" said Karl. "That means no one to tuck Karl in at night and read him a bedtime story." He eyed the Charmed Ones and smirked. "Unless one of you three would like to volunteer for the assignment."

Phoebe shuddered. "Can you say 'ewwww'?"

Suddenly, a cute, thin blonde popped over, light gleaming off her eyebrow, nose, and naval piercings, her hair in cornrows, wearing a tight, deep blue tank top ribbed with sky blue piping and sporting the number "42." Matching fingerless gloves reached up to just over her elbows, and a tattoo over her belly button showed a pair of diving dolphins and the words "So long and thanks for all the fish!"

The blonde nodded to the sisters, then turned to regard Karl with a look of distaste. "Personally, I'd rather cuddle with an anaconda than tuck you in at night, Karl. I have a feeling it would feel a lot more warm blooded!"

The sisters laughed, and Karl's condescending sneer remained firmly in place.

The pretty blonde held out her hand. "Jessica Harlowe, at your service. Consider Karl and me to be yin and yang. I'm into preserving the environment, he's into exploiting it and anyone and anything just to make a buck."

Karl shrugged. "Says the woman fending offers to transform her quaint little health food store in Reseda into an international chain."

"Yeah," Jessica said. "Fending off. As in 'shooing away.' As in 'get out of my face, Karl, I never liked you.'"

So Jess is all about the environment. Paige couldn't help but notice the way Jessica's gaze zeroed in, one by one, on all the hot guys at that party. *Huh, she's into hugging really old trees . . . and really young guys!*

A bespectacled brunette in a business suit with her hair pinned back bustled over to the scene. She was a *lot* younger up close than she had seemed at a distance, her prim-and-proper demeanor making her appear to be in her forties, not, as Paige now registered, barely twenty-five.

"All right, children, enough!" said the new-comer as she adjusted her tortoiseshell glasses. She nodded to the Charmed Ones. "Tamara Banks, official referee, it seems." Tamara regarded Karl and Jessica. "As much fun as it is to watch the unarmed attempt a battle of wits, this isn't your moment, either of you." She turned to their host. "Kevin?"

"Thank you, Tamara," he said. Then quickly he added, "Which is not to say that I agree with anything you said."

She nodded. "I'd have a coronary if you did." Grinning, Tamara aimed her thumb in Cassie's direction and said, "Invitation by association, in case you're wondering. I'm Cassie's friend."

Paige looked over to Cassie, and finally took notice of the guy next to her.

"Hello, Mr. Broody . . . ," Paige muttered quietly.

The man standing beside Cassie had hair that was dark and spiky, and had clearly partaken of product in a major way. His features were long and sharp, and in a strange way he reminded Paige of a character from a Japanese anime or manga, particularly his eyes, which seemed unusually big and round when he wished to appear friendly but could turn tiny and beady in a heartbeat. He wore his five o'clock shadow like a badge of honor, his goatee neat and reserved, his smile Mephisphelean. His black jacket and lime green tee had just sauntered off a fashion runway in Milan.

"I know who that is," Phoebe said. "Ryan Tobias. Heir to the Tobias Multinational fortune. All-around bad boy."

"Kinda reminds me of a thinner Colin Farrell," Piper noted.

Phoebe frowned. "Yeah, with an even worse rep for being a major-league bad boy. What's he doing with your pal's lady love?"

Paige shrugged. "I think he's some high-powered investment guy. Cassie must have brought him to help Kevin out."

Kevin called for everyone's attention. "First things first," Kevin said. "I want to take everyone on a tour of the house, and—"

Cassie's hand flashed high. "Hey, Kangaroo Kid!"

Kevin, the transplanted Australian, suddenly went pale. "Ah, uhm, Cass—Cuhh, Cassss . . . ," he stammered, and gasped.

"I know, I leave men speechless, it's my thing," she said with a bright laugh. Cassie shook her head. "Sorry, sweetie. You know I love you."

Kevin's eyebrows shot up in a forlorn needy-puppy expression. Paige could tell exactly how much he wanted to hear those words and have it not mean 'as a pal.' She looked around and wondered if anyone else had picked up on the signals.

"I just wanted to hog the spotlight for a second," Cassie said. "I'm sure everyone here knows that's not normally *my* thing. . . ."

Good-natured laughter abounded from the guests.

"I'd like to announce that there is a possibility that my wild and wanton days may soon be over. As much as I'm stunned to admit it—"

"You did it, just admit it!" roared the tightly knit group of unlikely pals in what was evidently an in-joke.

"—I think I've met the man of my dreams."

Kevin's jaw dropped. Paige could tell what he was thinking: Was it possible that Cassie would just declare her love for him right then and there in front of everyone? From what Paige remembered of what a spontaneous free spirit Cassie usually was, that seemed entirely possible.

Cassie gestured toward the handsome, dark-haired man next to her. "And here he is! Everyone, if you haven't met him yet, this is Ryan Tobias!"

Ryan raised his glass and smiled as nearly all the guests applauded.

Kevin's knees nearly buckled. Paige thought his heart might stop with shock. She rushed to his side, altogether conscious of the lovelorn way Kevin was staring at Cassie. Suddenly, Ryan's fingertips brushed Cassie's, their fingers entwined, their bodies followed, and with a sensuous ease, Ryan laid a passionate kiss on Cassie, which she returned.

Tamara frowned and shook her head disapprovingly. "It is the end of the world as we know it."

Paige whispered in Kevin's ear, "Are you okay?"

"Fine," he said quietly. But he held on to her for support.

Craig looked to Paige and Kevin with a sorrowful expression; he understood at once what was happening. In that moment, when Paige and Craig's gazes locked, a bond was formed. Though they were strangers, they would somehow join together to help their friend through this devastating disappointment.

Then Cassie finally appeared to register Kevin's distress, her gaze flickering from Ryan to Kevin and back again, almost as if she was suddenly undecided about her bold proclamation. Ryan saw the look—and his gaze turned cold and black.

Kevin raised his chin, planted his smile firmly in place, then went to greet his secret crush—and her boyfriend. Kevin held out his hand to the man who had won his wonderful Cassie's heart.

"I'm happy for you," Kevin said, forcing a smile into place.

Ryan shook his hand with a powerful grip and said, "That's not entirely true. After all, you don't know me, do you?"

"I, uh—" Kevin stammered, caught off guard.

Cassie elbowed Ryan in the ribs, but he deftly darted from the blow. "Hey!"

"I understand where you're coming from," Ryan said slyly. "Cassie told me all about the two of you."

"She did . . . ," Kevin murmured.

"Well, yeah!" Cassie said.

Ryan spoke in a deep and surprisingly gentle and introspective voice. "Absolutely. You're best friends. You might as well be brother and sister. So I know you want to look out for her, and frankly, I know I have a nasty reputation. It's totally deserved. I've done a lot of things I'm ashamed of. And you'd be crazy to just take my word for the fact that I've changed when, just three months ago, I was trashing hotel rooms *and* the reputations of pretty young things at Cannes."

Cassie rolled her eyes. "Like a lot of those women didn't know what they were in for. It still happens. They throw themselves at him just hoping to get their picture taken by the paparazzi. You wouldn't believe what we had to go through to make sure no photographers followed us here."

Ryan hugged Cassie close. "The point is, when I'm with Cassie, I feel like a different person. For the first time in my life I'm interested in what someone else has to say, not just the sound of my own voice. She's made me realize I *can* be a better person, so that's what I'm trying to do. I expect I'm going to stumble and fall a lot on the way, but I know she'll always be there to catch me."

Cassie blushed.

Paige drifted from the small group, realizing there was nothing more she could do for Kevin at that moment. She returned to her sisters, but kept an eye on her friend.

"Well, that's pretty much that, isn't it?" asked Piper. "I don't mean to be all gloom and doom about it or anything, but . . . look at those two. They're happy. They're in love. I'm sure Kevin isn't the kind of guy who'd selfishly stand in the way of something like that, no matter what feelings he has for Cassie."

Paige nodded. "You're right."

"Which means he might need some cheering up," Phoebe said, smacking her open palms together like it was time to go to work.

"Hey, hold up," Piper said, "Paige saw him first."

"Come on, stop it," Paige said. "He's my friend. I just want him to be happy. And I really don't think he's going to be interested in any other girl this weekend, you know?"

Phoebe smiled warmly. "Point."

"I just want to be there to support him however I can this weekend, that's all," Paige said, looking around for him.

Suddenly, Paige realized that Kevin was back onstage, dejectedly attempting to pick up where he had left off. Kevin rubbed his temples as if he had suddenly developed a throbbing migraine. "The house's, um, history . . . is interesting. It goes back for centuries, and—"

Suddenly, a hollow laugh erupted all around the partygoers.

A *ghostly* laugh . . .

If Paige hadn't known better, she might have thought that some supernatural form of the cavalry had arrived just in the nick of time to deflect attention away from Kevin and his evident pain and sorrow, and perhaps to restore some sense of fun to the festivities.

Craig stumbled back from a pair of French doors opening onto the pool area. He was breathless. "Who ordered the pirate ship?"

Kevin winced. "Pardon me?"

"Well, there's a pirate ship sitting in the pool out there and it wasn't there a couple of minutes ago," Craig said, pointing at the pool. "And—"

A voice sprang down from a third-floor balcony. "Avast, scurvy knaves!"

Paige and her sisters whirled to see a glowing, ghostly looking man wearing an elaborate pirate costume perched high above.

"I am the Pirate King!" announced the ghostly actor, who had decided to make his entrance. "And I come seeking booty!"

With another peel of laughter, he leaped into the air.

Chapter 4

The flying phantom was every inch the Hollywood ideal of an eighteenth-century pirate. His long black coat billowed out behind him like great wings, his frilly white shirt rippled, his enormous black leather boots gleamed, and his leather sash sailed across his chest to hold his shining sword. The audience gasped as he dropped, but his gloved hand shot out and snagged a dangling rope used to lower the chandeliers for cleaning.

With a triumphant "Hoo-hahhhhhh!" the supercharged spirit sped over their heads. It would have been quite an impressive stunt if he had managed to land right in front of the crowd. Instead, he suddenly whipped high and flew right smack into the wall behind them.

Into—and through it.

"Where'd he go?" asked Tamara.

"Duh!" yelped Jessica. "Ghost, remember?"

Tamara appeared shaken. "But there's no such thing!"

Craig sauntered to Kevin and clamped his hand on his pal's shoulder. "Where did you find this guy?" asked Craig with a hearty laugh. "I'd love to hire him to perform in my club."

"I didn't hire him," replied Kevin. "I don't know what's going on."

"I do!" Karl said drolly. "Someone was having lunch and they misplaced the *ham* from their sandwich!"

Suddenly, the pirate soared up from the hardwood floor, passing through it effortlessly, and grabbed Karl by the waist. Ghostly fingers curled around Karl's belt and hauled down his pants, exposing a pair of red and white boxers with huge Valentine's Day hearts.

The crowd exploded with laughter.

"What are you—a pirate or a circus clown!" demanded the outraged Karl as he struggled to yank his pants back up and regain some shred of his dignity.

Suddenly, the pirate went pale—and skeletal. Muck stole along its form, and its jaw dropped to incredible depths, its teeth suddenly filling with sharp, sharklike pointed teeth as it roared in terrifying abandon.

Piper whacked her forehead. "Oh, good, ya just *had* to tick it off, didn'tcha?"

The unearthly apparition straightened up, swallowed, and cleared his throat. He blinked and was completely flesh and blood once more. "Sorry, you're indeed correct, the pantsing was dead on, but the graveyard bit . . . quite uncalled for. Take two!"

He vanished, then reappeared high upon the balcony, where he had first been spotted. With a cry of adventure he leaped again, the rope magically appearing when he needed it most, and this time he dropped down directly before Cassie.

Piper watched the ghost closely. She could see the spectral pirate's long black hair and beard move, as if brushed by an ocean breeze, and she could almost smell salt air. Beyond the pirate, Piper had a view out of the dining room toward the pool, and sure enough, an enormous, creaking and swaying Spanish galleon was docked there.

"You thought you might escape me, villain!" shouted the dread pirate king as he thrust a finger toward Ryan. "I shall rescue my beloved Henrietta and we shall be gone before any of your men can follow us."

The pirate winked at Cassie and scooped her up in his arms. "Come, my love," called the pirate. "Let us away."

"Whoa!" she said with a peel of laughter as her hands settled on his ectoplasmic flesh. "Chilly!"

"I'm sure you can warm me up, wench!" he growled happily. "Just like old times!"

Ryan finally shook himself from his shock and strode forward. "Hey, hold on, pal, she's—"

The Pirate King shook his head, his ghostly eyes bulging. "Too late to play the part of the gallant, Commodore Ryan, you dark-spirited fiend. We know each other too well for that."

Ryan's gaze narrowed, and he reached for the ghost—

But a high, piercing chittering sounded in the hall, the shrill, unexpected sound making Ryan leap back. A barrel dropped from the ceiling and splintered beside the pirate. From it, a dozen, two dozen, no, three dozen or more screeching monkeys wearing the brilliant clothes of pirates, eye patches, and tiny wooden parrots arrived. They even carried small swords.

"Sea monkeys," Phoebe said. "Nice one!"

The spirit spirited Cassie away on the rope that had again magically appeared in its time of need and swung her to the stage as the legion of upset monkeys formed a ring around Ryan and menacingly converged on him.

The ghost bent down to kiss her and suddenly stopped himself. "You're not Henrietta," he said, startled. He shook his head and squinted. He whipped out a pair of bifocals, peered through them, and rolled his eyes. "Blast! I knew I should have gotten my eyes examined before planning my daring rescue."

Piper watched the sea monkeys back Ryan into a corner. Her gaze whipped about to the other laughing partygoers.

"Shouldn't we do something?" Phoebe asked.

"I'm not sure what to do," stated Piper flatly. "If there are Innocents in danger, we save them, this I know. The only thing these Innocents are in danger of is witnessing some hammy over-acting."

"We'd better do something before Ryan over there gets a taste o' monkey lovin' from those frisky fritters!" Paige declared.

The pirate vanished from the stage and reappeared before the Charmed Ones.

"*There* you are, my beloved," the pirate cooed. "Now I shall take you away from all this."

"You mean I'll never have to do dishes ever again?" Paige quipped.

With that, the pirate snatched Paige and vanished with her.

Piper's eyes shot open wide in alarm. "Where's Paige?"

"You worry about her. I'm going to lend Ryan some moral support with the sea monkeys," Phoebe vowed. She stormed at the besieged Ryan and barked, "All right, you little blighters, time to straighten up and fly right, or whatever ghostly pirate sea monkeys do!"

The monkeys scattered at her determined approach—and swarmed over the snack table. With a shrill series of shrieks, they grabbed at escargot, calamari, pineapple squares, and chocolate truffles and lobbed their discoveries at Ryan and Phoebe.

"Now that's just wrong!" Ryan yelled, raising his designer jacket as a shield.

Phoebe ducked behind it with him. "Well, they *are* monkeys. There are worse things they could be throwing."

Paige and the ghost rematerialized atop the longest and nearest dinner table. Paige looked down and saw that her funky little micro-mini and sequined halter had vanished. Not that she was suddenly in the altogether, either. In fact, her clothes had been transformed into sexy lady pirate wear, including a red velvet corset and pants with a white lace blouse and a bandanna.

She saw Piper quickly approaching and put her hand out. "I got this one!"

"Do you really think so?" asked the ghost, raising his saber. He reached for her, and she shrugged off his ghostly grip.

What happened a moment ago? Paige wondered, feeling slightly disoriented. *We disappeared and . . . went somewhere? A dressing room? And . . . did I have lines to rehearse?*

"Unhand me!" shouted Paige, suddenly remembering her lines and getting into the part. "No man shall have me unless he can best me with the sword."

Paige turned on the pirate and hollered, "Sword!"

A dazzling rune-covered blade magically materialized in her hand. The ghost raised an eyebrow. "Where'd that come from? You're already armed with a cutlass."

Uh-oh, Paige realized, *I just used magic in front of everybody. Oh, well, they'll just figure it's part of the act, even the ghost acting surprised.*

Paige looked down at the scabbard slapping against her hip. "Cutlasses are for wusses. I'm a fiery sea-wench, and this is a Nordic-Edge 3000. Top o' the line, matey, prepare to meet thy doom!"

She jabbed the point against his throat, and the pirate laughed in delight.

"May I just say one thing?" asked the Pirate King. "Woof!"

Whipping her wild auburn hair free of her bandanna, Pirate Paige attacked. The ghost's bold attacks and feints checked the shimmering sweep of her sword. Steel met steel in a shower of sparks, Paige's biting blade flashing and driving the pirate forward to the end of the table as the partygoers looked on, including Phoebe and Ryan. They'd been released by the curious monkeys, who also wanted to see the fight.

"Paige, do you have any idea what you're doing?" called the worried Phoebe. "You've never had sword training!"

"Really?" Paige asked, watching her hand lash the sword wildly one way, then the other in a frenzied, expert blur. "Coulda fooled me."

A bold whoosh of striking swords cleaved the air, and an instant before the ghost might have teetered off the table's edge, he growled and rushed at Paige, his sword driving through her.

His sword—and all the rest of his immaterial form. She shivered. "That was chilly!"

"See?" Cassie demanded, folding herself back into Ryan's waiting arms. Kevin could only watch.

"Give it up, pal!" Paige called as the battle resumed. "You'll never take me alive! Just concentrate on your other ill-gotten gains."

"Ah, yes, my dear," he countered, casually swiping the air with his blade. "But all the treasure in the world could not compare with the shining beauty and elegance that you reward me with. A kiss, my dear? A single kiss? And then I might pass on happily, to my final reward."

"Hah!" she cried zestily.

Paige and the pirate swashed their buckles, the witch's eyes sparkling with pleasure. Sensing the time was right to put an end to the show, Paige feinted to the right while the Pirate King thrust hard to the left. They collided, the Pirate King taking her into his arms, their swords falling, clamoring to the cool oak of the table below.

Paige didn't resist. Feeling like a heroine in a romance novel, she allowed him to pull her to him and kiss her passionately on the lips, liquid fire erupting at the touch of the tip of his ghostly tongue. Unearthly tingles shot through her.

Whoa, now here's a guy who knows how to kiss, Paige thought as they gently parted.

"You're a delightful bonny lass," he declared. In her ear, he whispered, "That's a very good and kind thing you're attempting to do for your friend."

Paige couldn't believe it. The ghost *had* chosen exactly that moment to strike with his shenanigans so that he might ride to Kevin's rescue. She looked to her friend and saw that Kevin was calm and composed once more. Saddened, but no longer a wreck.

"Now that I have what I want, I shall take my leave," said the Pirate King. "But if you ever need me, my dear, you just have to whistle. You *do* know how to whistle, don't you?"

And with those words the Pirate King faded away, leaving Paige standing alone, whistling to herself.

"We've got ourselves *one* friendly ghost," she muttered as memory of that passionate kiss with the spirit washed over her. "And then some!"

She looked around—and the partygoers exploded with applause.

After the excitement had died down, Paige had been given time to go upstairs with her sisters to shower and change. Piper and Phoebe were waiting in Paige's bedroom as she emerged from the bath wearing a silk robe, and a fluffy white towel around her reddish locks.

Piper grinned as she took in the room's opulence. "It looks like Saint Valentine's Day exploded in here!"

It was true. The vast, oval-shaped room was done up in the style of Louis XVI, everything in red and white. All the furniture had slender, reedlike legs and delicate swag or scroll motifs. The inlaid-kingwood bed from the 1700s was dwarfed by the sheer size of the room, and the kidney-shaped rosewood parquetry table, from the 1800s, featured brass mounts. Red damask upholstery and wall coverings, as well as the lightly patterned Aubusson carpets, contributed to the room's refined yet passionate look.

"More interested in what went on downstairs," Paige said, furiously drying her hair. "Anyone spot the monkeys after all the ruckus died down?"

"Gone like the pirate ship and all the other props," Piper said. "Ghost guy puts on a heck of a show!"

"Got to admit," Paige said, sitting down on the bed, "that was something you don't experience every day."

Piper shrugged. "No, not unless you're *us*."

"Point," admitted Paige. "I suppose if any of us had any doubts that there really is a haunting—or something—going on here, well, they're out the window now."

"You mean like a certain fire-haired, man-crazy pirate wench's virtue?" teased Phoebe.

"Don't even go there," Paige warned. "Yes, I just made out with a ghost. Talk about taking one for the team, sheesh. . . ."

Piper grinned. "Sucking face with a ghost . . . actually, considering who I'm married to, you could say that I do that a lot. Your guy any good?"

"Not bad, actually," Paige had to admit.

Phoebe wandered to a small table and examined a leather-bound script book from the days of Shakespeare at the Globe Theatre. "It's interesting," Phoebe said. "Did you notice how much fun everyone was having? Especially the ghost, or whatever it was?"

Piper nodded. "Yeah, it was like the more everyone got into it, the more over-the-top the antics became. Still, I'm not sure it wasn't meant to scare us off. I always think, the ghost says 'Get out of the house,' maybe people should consider, oh, I dunno, wait for it—getting out of the house!"

Paige shook her head. "No, you've got him all wrong. Don't you get it? The ghost isn't trying to scare anyone off. He's putting on a show and he wants an audience. He just wants the right kind of audience."

"Continue . . . ," Piper invited.

Paige plopped down on the bed and studied the elaborate mural painted upon the ceiling. It depicted a host of heavenly creatures performing on a stage for a mass of otherunworldly types. "I betcha that if we went back through every one of those incidents with the ghost really working hard to make people's lives miserable so they'd leave, each one would come back to people trying to change the house. Even today, the band was in there with their own electricians, messing around with the house's wiring to give themselves more juice, and the events coordinator and the caterer had their own people moving furniture, going at it with hammers and drills to add fixtures and stuff. . . . The ghost wasn't loving it, and he let his feelings be known."

"So if Kevin tries to remodel, he's had it?" asked Phoebe.

Paige rolled over and propped herself up on one elbow. The bed was so comfortable! "Kevin loves this place just the way it is. I don't think he even knew half that stuff was going on until it was too late."

"Bottom line," said Piper, "no one here thinks they were really seeing a ghost. They're convinced it was all actors and special effects and crazy stuff Kevin's pulling to entertain everyone."

"Kevin doesn't have a clue what's going on either," Paige added, "but he isn't wigged or anything. He thinks it's cool. I figure I'll encourage him to believe the whole thing's some crazy present from the suits at the studio."

"Cool," said Phoebe, her brow knitting with concentration. "Well, I think it's high time we looked into the ghostly goings-on. If Kevin's serious about living here, then it sounds like something needs to be done."

"I'm good with that," Piper said. "Tell you what, I'll start hunting around looking for talismans or any other objects that might be physical anchors, keeping the ghost bound to the house. Y'know, hidden chambers where stuff might be stashed, old bones that need to be dug up and replanted in consecrated ground, the usual."

"Wait, wait, wait!" Phoebe said. "We don't know this is a ghost."

Piper looked at her sister as if she suddenly had two heads . . . which had probably been the case at some time or another during all their time battling evil. "What else would it be?"

"Uh—demon?" Phoebe countered. "One kind of evil masquerading as another? We've seen it before lots of times. This is a perfect setup. The place is empty just about all the time, a big sprawling mansion where you could house dozens of demons planning big nasty demony-stuff. They take advantage of all the hysteria surrounding the place, the tall tales about spirits haunting the place, and they use their powers to make it look haunted now and then when they need to."

"Huh," Piper said, swinging her long hair back with a sigh. "So that creative writing course you were taking is starting to pay off."

Phoebe rolled her eyes. "Hardy-har."

Piper tossed up her hands. "I'm just saying, if it walks like a duck and quacks like a duck, you better believe its last name is gonna be à l'orange. Heck, it could even be one or more of the guests here in disguise. I plan on finding out."

Paige eased over to her wardrobe and selected a fresh outfit. Her pirate garb was hanging up in the bathroom. "Listen, you guys deal with the ghost, or demon, or whatever's here, if there really is anything here at all. I'm gonna try to help Kevin."

In another bedroom far down the hall, Ryan stared into an ancient mirror. He stood alone, grateful that no one was there to see how truly shaken the experience downstairs had left him.

Staring deeply into the glass, he gasped as he suddenly glimpsed a faint glimmering of light deep within its depths. A rising tide of darkness suffused his reflection, and in his mind, Ryan heard whispers, sweet tempting voices luring him with promises of power, of control over his family's empire, and so much more. . . .

The overhead light flickered on and Ryan darted from the glass, drawing in a sharp, pained breath as he whirled to face Karl.

"Hard to see anything in the dark," Karl commented, closing the door behind him and sealing the two of them in together.

I'm not so sure about that, Ryan thought, his gaze drifting back to the ancient mirror.

"Cassie?" asked Karl.

"Partying with that she-vixen Tamara," Ryan told him.

Karl laughed and pulled up an antique wood-carved chair. "Plotting your downfall and mine, if I know Tamara."

"Probably," Ryan said. "But Cassie's not that easily swayed. She'll listen to advice, but she goes with what her heart tells her."

"Good for you," Karl said. "Not so much for her."

Ryan sighed. "What do you want?"

Smiling, Karl said, "Money, power, control. Same as you. And I hate to miss out on an opportunity."

"Go on . . ."

"That spookshow downstairs was beyond belief," Karl said. "I mean that literally. I don't believe it had anything at all to do with ghosts."

"Neither do I," Ryan ventured, though his tone was less than convincing.

"I think there's some kind of experimental technology being tested out here," Karl added. "Hard light holography taken to a level never even dreamed of before. Smoke and mirrors like no one's business."

"Your point?"

"I want a cut of it!" Karl roared. "And so should you. This could be exactly the discovery you need to finally carve your own niche in your family's empire. The technology must be right here, in the walls, the floors, the ceilings. And no matter what he says, Kevin is at the heart of it. He must be. And his little red-haired pal too!"

"Something's here," Ryan said, his gaze drifting back to the mirror. "You're right about that. Something that, yes, I think I want a part of."

And from downstairs, the sounds of a party drifted toward them.

Paige met Kevin in the mansion's well-appointed study. The exquisite rug at their feet had been hand-woven in India with an Ispahan pattern, and the wood-paneled study sported a fireplace carved from Tavernell marble. The casual opulence of Maxwell Manor was astonishing.

"So how are you doing?" Paige asked.

"I don't know," Kevin admitted. "Finding out about Cassie and Ryan . . . that was one big kick in the head. But I want Cassie to be happy, and if this guy's the one, then that's all that matters."

Paige nodded, astonished by his lack of selfishness. Of course, she had come to a similar conclusion about the two of them in the restaurant. Did this revelation that Cassie was in love with Ryan reopen the possibility that she and Kevin might become a couple again? No, not anytime soon, possibly not ever. As much as Kevin was a stunner, and one of the sweetest souls Paige had ever known, his heart would always belong to Cassie.

"How are *you* holding up?" he asked sweetly. "You're the one who just dueled with a ghost."

"Fine," she said. "Wondering how *whoever's* behind this pulled it off, but enjoying myself."

Kevin nodded. "I think that if the ghost of Robert Maxwell really is in this house somewhere, that's what he'd most want to hear."

"I concur, Counselor," she said with a bold laugh.

Together they returned to the dining room, where music blared from Cassie's stereo. Ryan swung in behind him, Karl joining a moment later.

Craig also swung in and greeted Kevin.

"Wasn't that awesome?" Craig said, clapping his pal on the back. "Oh, man, I don't ever want to leave this place. Kevin, I don't know how you pulled it off, but that was amazing. Where are you hiding those guys?"

"What guys?" asked Kevin.

"The actors who played the pirates and all the techs. That lead dude was so funny, I could book him as a headliner at the comedy club tomorrow."

"Well, they're all pretty busy, actually," Paige said, cutting in.

Craig nodded. "Ah. Union talent. Say no more."

A strange smell drifted from the kitchen, and Craig quickly excused himself.

"Um, nice save, thanks," Kevin said.

"No problem," Paige said, pecking Kevin on the cheek as she saw him eye Cassie worriedly.

Steeling himself, Kevin stepped forward and addressed his guests once more. "So, I promised you fun and games. As you can see, they've already begun. Now it's time to crank it up a little. Everyone? We're going on a ghost hunt!"

Cheers rose up from the partygoers, which now included all three Charmed Ones.

"So let's set up the ground rules," Kevin declared. "The first rule is that while, yes, we can cover more ground and look for more clues about why and how Robert Maxwell is haunting this house if we each went our separate ways, that's not what we're gonna do. We stick together in groups, and we don't let ourselves be separated for any reason. I've already drawn up group assignments, and they're final, so no whining."

Kevin surveyed the eager faces of his guests. "Second rule, do no harm. The ghost is very protective of the house and everything in it. I think Maxwell's a fun guy who's not going to mind us poking around a little so long as we're respectful. Cross that line, though, and things might get a little out of hand. So don't do that! Otherwise, have fun, and let's meet up here in two hours."

The partygoers surged forward and snatched the group assignments from Kevin. There were whines and moans, but everyone quickly settled into the spirit of the thing.

So to speak.

Piper frowned as she looked at her assignment sheet and huddled with her sisters. "Wait a second, did you see the way these lists are broken down? We're all in different groups. It's going to be almost impossible for us to do anything about the ghost business unless it's just the three of us together with no prying eyes to see something magical."

"I don't see the ghost as that big a problem," Paige contended. "He helped Kevin, and that's what I need to be doing too. I'm sorry, but I really need to let you guys deal with this on your own, if that's okay."

"You bet." Phoebe said. "We ain't afraid of no ghosts."

"Speak for yourself," Piper said. "I'm a little nervous about this one's fashion sense. But we won't go there."

Paige went to Kevin and Tamara while her sisters continued to playfully conspire.

"Look, we're not supposed to wander away on our own," Piper said, "but we're all grown-ups, you know everyone's gonna do it, let's just settle on a plan for vanquishing this ghost and—"

"But he's friendly!" Phoebe protested. "He, or it, whatever's going on."

"The jury's still out, so far as I'm concerned," Piper said. "I've seen spirits turn on a dime, and so have you. Maybe this one's just acting nice and friendly to get us to lower our guard, and then who knows? I'd rather be ready for it."

Phoebe shrugged. What could she say? She was the one who had suggested demonic activity as a real possibility in the house. If she was right, vanquishing would be in order, big-time!

The Charmed Ones split up and joined their assigned groups.

"A ghost-hunting we will go," Phoebe sang happily. The group made their way into the sprawling hallway and into the unknown.

Chapter 5

Paige prowled the halls with Kevin, Craig, and Tamara. She'd hardly had any time alone with Tamara, who was something of a curiosity to her. This seemed like such an odd group to have been the key friends who supported Kevin through the years, and she was anxious to hear all their stories.

They drifted to the music room together, each examining the eighteenth-century harpsichord that—rumor had it—had once been played by Mozart. Along one wall were framed compositions that were either written at the mansion or inspired by one of the owners. The final wall was decorated with two tapestries. The first showed Prometheus giving fire to the first human beings, the second depicted Prometheus being tortured by the gods for his gift.

"So, Cassie and Ryan," Paige casually mentioned. "They seem happy."

"I think Cassie's making the biggest mistake of her life," Tamara said flatly.

"Really," Paige murmured. "So you think there's someone else who'd be better for Cassie?"

Tamara the businesswoman turned and fixed Paige with a withering stare. "No. I think the concept of romantic love is nothing but a ploy created by big businesses and governments to help encourage an economy of out-of-control spending and to help keep the masses miserable and docile. I think Cassie should be free to play with any boy toy she sets her mind on, but settling down with *anyone*? She might as well lie down and die."

"Oh!" Paige chirped. "Glad we cleared that up."

Tamara drifted from the room as Craig breezed in. He took one look at the tapestries and said, "Harsh."

Paige nodded. "Totally."

They laughed, and Paige asked Craig, "How'd you meet Kevin?"

Craig grinned. "Yah really wanna know?"

Piper sensed a great story coming on. "I do."

He sighed. "I used to be in what we call the clothing removal business."

"A male stripper?" she asked, not all that incredulously, considering his major-league hot bod.

"Yup," he said. "So here's the deal. I was

hired to deliver a strip-o-gram to this lady at the insurance company one floor above the newspaper where Kev was working. I show up, ready to go to work, and I'm riding up the elevator to do the job. It's really crowded, pretty much full to capacity, a whole ton of us are just crammed in like sardines."

"Including Kevin?"

"Including Kevin, whom I didn't know at the time," Craig explained. "The elevator stops, we're not at my floor yet, but there's this pregnant lady, and she's about to step on. Now it's already packed, so I'm thinking, okay, I'm going to step out and take the next one so she can get in. Then I see what I'm totally certain she doesn't: the elevator didn't come down all the way, there's a four- or five-inch gap, and I think pretty mama pregnant lady's about to step down to her doom, so I leap for it. And wham, I trip, sprawl, nearly take her down with me, and twist my ankle doing it. And it turns out, she had seen it, she was trying to warn *me* because it looked to her like I was going to go flying out of there like a boneheaded maniac, which is exactly what I did."

She laughed. "Nice . . ."

"Yeah. Kevin sees the whole thing, he's the only one who realizes I'm actually hurt, everyone else is laughing their heads off. He gets off, checks out my ankle, starts letting me know all this medical stuff he learned from doing articles from medical newsletters. He tells me I'm out of luck, it's a nasty sprain, no way I'm delivering the S.O.G."

"S.O.G.?"

His brilliant smile flashed in the music room. He reached out and plucked the harp's strings. "Strip-o-gram."

"Right!"

"You know what he does?" asked Craig.

"Besides calling a paramedic and a good trip-and-fall attorney for you?"

"He went on in my place," Craig told her. "I was lying there on the rug, cursing up a storm, saying how that was it for me, I was going to get fired for this, it was my third screwup in three weeks . . . and he just gave me his cell so I could make the call to the paramedics and he went up and did the job. Later on, he even gave me his tips!"

"You should have let him keep those."

"I tried, but you know Kevin. He gets an idea in his head, there's no stopping him. Ever since that day, man, I'd walk through fire for that guy, jump into traffic, whatever it took. I've got family I'm not that close to, you know what I mean? And without his help and encouragement, I never would have gotten my comedy club. You know what I called it?"

Paige shook her head.

"Kev's."

"That's awesome," she said at last. Her brow

furrowed in confusion, and she peeked out into the hall. Kevin and Tamara were walking off on their own, discussing something animatedly. Paige followed them out, Craig at her heels.

Suddenly, halfway down the hall, Paige felt a brush of icy lips on the nape of her neck.

"Head's up, hide quick!" urged a familiar, ghostly voice. It was Maxwell!

Paige snatched up Craig's hand and slipped into a nook with him behind a suit of armor. Looking out into the hall, Paige was surprised to find it empty. So much for the groups sticking together. *Huh. I wonder why Maxwell wanted me to hide?*

Next to Paige, Craig grinned and said, "Isn't this rather sudden? We hardly know each other!"

With a warm smile, she lightly punched his shoulder and said, "Cut the clowning around, you! We've got some serious business to discuss."

"I know," he said softly, his expression turning serious. "How do you think Kevin's holding up?"

"Right now?" Paige sighed. "So far, so good. I'm more worried about what happens on Monday when *we're* all gone and he's got nothing to do but brood in this big empty house." She considered her options and added, "Maybe I can stick around longer."

Even as those words left her lips, she was all

too aware that her duties as a Charmed One would probably not allow for her to be away from her sisters for long. Of course, she could orb back and forth at a moment's notice. Kevin was so distracted that explaining her disappearances would be a piece of cake.

"He'll have plenty of work to focus on," Craig assured her. "That'll keep him—"

Suddenly, two more bodies pressed in on them in the little hidey-hole behind the suit of armor. Paige and Craig flattened against the wall, and pressed even closer together, which wasn't a bad thing so far as she was concerned. . . .

Okay, so this is why the ghost was warning me, Paige realized.

The two newcomers who had stolen into the nook hadn't even spotted them in the shadows, although Paige and Craig were close enough to lean forward and breathe down their necks.

It was Ryan and Karl.

"I don't think this is a good time or place for a chitchat," Karl spat. "Kevin and that woman are just down the hall."

"They're too busy to notice us," Ryan said. "All right, I was thinking about what you said before, about getting ahold of whatever Kevin is using to make us think the place is haunted. I agree, it would be terrific to snag the rights, but there's a more pressing issue: Cassie."

"I thought you would have proposed to her already," Karl said in a hushed tone.

Ryan snickered. "I like that word. Proposing. Makes it sound as if the outcome isn't completely certain."

"I just mean . . ."

"She works in a comic shop," Ryan said cruelly. "I have my own jet. Like there's any chance she's going to say no."

"You own your own jet right *now*," Karl reminded him. "And a helicopter, a townhouse in Vienna, a controlling share in my company—"

"Your point is?"

"The press has been tearing you to pieces over the last year," Karl reminded him. "Dating Wonder Woman definitely turned things around, but they haven't fully expunged the public memory of your string of regrettable incidents up to that point. Your parents have made their position clear. Marry this one, or you're cut off. And then all those things you say you own, well . . . we know who really signed the leases, don't we?"

"Father," Ryan growled. "Whom you will go tattling to at the slightest provocation."

"Indeed I will. *I* know who signs *my* checks. They pay me to be your friend, your confidant, your assistant with matters less lofty than you like, and to come up with platitudes and humble bits of dialogue for you to drop here and there to make you sound almost human. I'm here to protect their interests and yours. So what's your plan?"

"Of course I'm going to take care of it this weekend, but I'm putting it off as long as possible," Ryan said. "Otherwise, all these losers will be clucking here and there, making a fuss. Who needs that? Cassie and I are having dinner with my parents Sunday evening. I'll hit her with the rock just before we get out of here Sunday afternoon."

Whoa, thought Paige as Karl and Ryan drifted by her place of concealment. *This guy hasn't changed one bit. He just got a better speechwriter.*

"But I think Kevin's going to be a problem," Ryan said. "It looks like one of those pathetic 'I've always loved you from afar' routines, and it couldn't be coming at a worse time. Our goal needs to be twofold: We need to discredit him in Cassie's eyes so that when it comes time to bite the bullet and propose on Sunday, she won't even think of saying no to me. At the same time, we need to get ahold of a controlling interest in whatever technology he's using."

"What did you have in mind?" Karl asked excitedly.

"There were some incidents earlier today, correct? Some of this ridiculous ghost business where someone could have easily broken their neck? We can use that for inspiration. . . ."

Karl shook his head. "Wait, I'm not going to be a part of anyone ending up in the hospital— or the morgue."

"It won't come to that," Ryan assured him. "It

won't need to. I've got the whole thing forming in my head, but I'll need your help to pull it off."

"Done."

The plotting pair stole off down the corridor. After they had left, Paige realized how tightly she'd been pressed up against Craig and exactly how good it had felt.

I'm not man-crazy, not-not-not! she swore to herself. *Even when the man in question has muscles like steel girders and the cutest little dimples I've ever seen.*

Paige peeked out and saw that the conspirators were long gone. She whispered, "Well, that puts things in a new light, now doesn't it?"

"Um-hmmm," added Craig. "The question is: What do we do about it?"

"Keep an eye on those two, figure out exactly what their plan is, and make sure it blows up in their faces," Paige vowed. "Operation Kevin and Cassie is totally back on!"

Craig grinned. "Paige, I like your style."

"Why, thank you, good sir," she said appreciatively. "Honestly, though—what's not to like?"

Up on the third floor, Piper had lost track of Karl and Ryan, and that was just fine with her; she didn't like either of them. Plus, she had a job to do. She was convinced that this haunting was exactly what it looked like, and tonight she planned on proving it.

Double-checking to be sure that no one was near her, Piper crossed her arms over her chest and tapped her toes impatiently. "Yo, ghost guy! This is what they call a friendly summons. No spells, no tricks. Just get your ectoplasmic backside out here so we can have a chitchat about your intentions."

She waited. After a while, it looked like she would be waiting a good long time, possibly forever. "Last chance!" she called. "We can do this the easy way or the hard way, it's your choice."

Suddenly, she heard the unmistakable padding of feline footsies closing in from around a bend in the corridor.

"I didn't know Kevin had cats," she mused. The soft, gently running motor sound of a kitty cat's purr echoed from the end of the hall. The padding of paws, the clicking of claws, both drew closer and became louder.

Much, *much* louder.

"What the blue blazes?" Piper muttered. The hairs on her neck suddenly stood up, and her senses kicked into overdrive as a shadow stretched toward her as "kitty" finally appeared . . . all five hundred pounds of her! The giant cat had sleek black silky fur, twin gleaming emeralds for eyes, and darksome lips that pulled back as it hissed to reveal sharp, glistening fangs. The cat's jaws opened wide enough to swallow Piper whole with one bite.

"Aw, heck!" Piper hollered, suddenly wishing

she had slipped on her running shoes. *Flats!* she thought as she spun and bolted, the towering feline hungrily bounding after her, its claws swiping the air that only moments earlier had contained her long dark tresses. *Why don't I ever learn? Flats are the rage for these kinds of festivities, flats!*

Piper stumbled on her boot heels, fell and flipped onto her back, and jammed her open hands up toward the fearsome feline. "I don't want to do this, I like kitty cats," she moaned, wincing as she smelled its fetid breath. She stared into its face and saw a look of triumph as the predator raised a claw and surged forward, jaws open wide.

Striking without hesitation, Piper blew the apparition to bits. Only . . . the *bits* didn't want to stay blown apart. They quickly re-formed, and the giant cat whose head brushed against the ceiling hissed again even as Piper bounded to her feet and broke into another run.

Chapter 6

Phoebe and her companions surveyed the mansion's vast conservatory. Constructed of glass and stone, filled to overflowing with exotic jungle plants, the conservatory radiated beauty and supernatural intrigue.

"Were all these plants placed here for this weekend?" asked Jessica, the environmentalist. "Who takes care of them?"

Cassie grinned. "Maybe the ghost has a green thumb."

Phoebe smiled faintly at that. *The ghost or whatever it is I've been sensing in this creepy old place . . .*

They passed rattan and bamboo furniture that added to the room's otherworldly feel, and stopped before a gloriously designed marble fountain that held a statue of the four muses. Each of the muses looked out at a different point in the compass and held in their hand the symbol of the creative ideas that they might deliver to the creative mind. Rumor had it that Rudyard Kipling had once written a short story in this room because it reminded him so much of India.

Phoebe eyed her companions carefully and thought, *If I'm right, and there is something more than just a friendly ghost in this house, then maybe whatever's really behind the "hauntings" is masquerading as one of the guests.*

She eyed Cassie and Jessica carefully. It could be anyone. . . .

Phoebe caught up to Jessica and said, "So you and Kevin go way back, huh?"

"Isn't he just a dream?" asked Jessica as her fingers absently transformed a napkin from a small serving table into an origami tiger. "I used to work at Latte Latitudes in L.A., back before I really found out about organic foods and being one with the environment. Kevin—poor guy— was *always* strapped for cash. I used to give him free lattes all the time, and he thought it was because I'm this naturally kind and giving person and stuff. Man, I just thought he was a hottie!"

Phoebe laughed. *Yeah, sure,* you're *a demon in disguise. Sheesh!*

"Anyway, Kev has been great," Jessica said, casually working more and more detail into the paper tiger. "He helped me make my dream come true and go from working as a clerk at Health Nuts to owning my own place. He's the best."

"Absolutely," Cassie added absently.

Jessica flipped the paper tiger high, and Phoebe looked down as it floated into her hands. By the time she looked up again, Jessica was walking beside Cassie, and together they were vanishing into the hall.

Phoebe turned to follow them, her hand absently brushing the table. Gasping, she drew it back sharply as if she'd been stung by a scorpion's tail. In Maxwell Manor, ectoplasmic emanations thrummed and throbbed in the bricks and mortar, the stone and steel that was the house's breadth and body, and there was no way that one ghost could be powerful enough to give this house the power it possessed. Something else was clearly going on here—but what?

Cassie suddenly stopped and shivered. She drew back and cried, "Whoa!"

Phoebe raced along the hall to her side. "What happened?"

"I was just walking along and I hit this spot and it was *freezing*," Cassie explained as Jessica caught up to them. "I was freezing, it felt like—"

"A cold spot," Phoebe said quickly. "It's one of those traditional things with hauntings." Phoebe walked over to the spot and held her hand out. Sure enough, it was as if she'd plunged her fingers into a bucket of ice. She whipped her hand back and looked around. There were no air-conditioning vents or anything else that would explain how or why this small space in the hall could turn a person into a Popsicle if they stood there long enough.

An eerie haunting melody suddenly sounded from a room up ahead.

Cassie grinned. "Wow, Kevin really goes all out, doesn't he? A cold spot, now this."

"*Someone's* going all out," Phoebe whispered suspiciously. "Someone wants to convince us this place really is haunted and that's all there is to it. . . ."

They came to the door, which was partially ajar, and pushed it open. "The music's coming from here," Phoebe called as she entered the empty chamber.

"Probably some speakers in the wall," Cassie said. "Neat trick!"

"Makes sense," added Jessica.

Suddenly, something reached down from the darkness above and snagged Phoebe's hair. It twisted and yanked savagely, nearly lifting her from her feet. She yelped, looked up—

Nothing, there was nothing to see. Whatever had grabbed her then released her just as quickly.

Cassie stared wide-eyed at Phoebe. "Your hair just shot straight up and then fell. How the—"

"Static electricity?" Jessica speculated. "Or maybe just super bad mojo."

Phoebe eyed her companions once more as she brushed at her bruised scalp. *If either of these two is in on whatever's really going on here, they're doing a great job of covering their tracks,* Phoebe thought.

Phoebe warily led them back to the hall, suddenly aware of exactly how on edge the hair-pulling incident had made them all. When she had been grabbed, Phoebe felt as if something cold, dark, and malevolent had struck at her, anxious to toy with her, harm her, even. The feeling was unlike anything that she had sensed when the spectral Pirate King had put on his show in the dining room.

Phoebe wondered, *What if Maxwell's ghost really is here . . . but even he doesn't realize that some other supernatural entity has also come here?*

Soon, the house became a fun house once more. While exploring another room looking for clues, Cassie glanced out the window and drew in a sharp breath. Phoebe raced to her side and peered through the window—

The house was now on the sea.

"What the . . . ," whispered Jessica as she looked over their shoulders.

Phoebe's eyes widened at the sight. She darted to another window, and outside, the chopping, rolling waves of the sea splattered up around the house's walls, obscuring all else. They raced to a window in another room across the hall and it was exactly the same.

Then a sudden roar of water raced down the hall and the blaring sounds of sixties surfer music rose up. A spectral figure wearing baggy Day-Glo swim trunks sailed by, riding the crest of a wave that splashed and splattered along the corridors as the women watched in wonder.

"Surf's up!" cried Maxwell's ghost. "Catch me if you can, ghost-hunters. Woo-hoo!"

Phoebe saw the crash coming and called, "Look out for that—"

Maxwell smashed against the far wall, dematerializing along with his board and the wave itself. When Phoebe whirled to the window, she saw that the view of the apple grove had returned.

"Wicked!" Cassie cried, loving the show.

Soon, the trio was carefully treading to the end of the corridor. They hung a right and suddenly realized that they had seen the painting beside them at the end of the previous corridor.

"Two identical paintings, that's weird," Phoebe muttered.

In fact, many things were the exact same between this corridor and the last one they had been down. The doors ahead were locked, and a feeling at their backs urged them on, as if something scary was behind them and they didn't dare look back.

"I've got goose bumps," Cassie said excitedly.

Phoebe smiled. *Cassie really has a sense of adventure,* Phoebe thought, smiling. *I can see why Kevin's so into her.*

The witch could see that it was getting darker

behind her, the shadows at her feet lengthening. The group pressed forward and again encountered the same painting. But now the corridor at the end of the hall split in two directions, yet when the women reached it, they saw creepy shadows stalking toward them from both directions.

Phoebe looked up and realized another corridor lie directly ahead. She darted toward it—and smacked something cold and hard, bouncing back to land right on her butt.

Ghostly laughter filtered down around her. "See?" asked the ghost. "It's not so funny when you're the one running into things!"

Tell that to these two, Phoebe thought as she picked herself up while Cassie and Jessica fell together laughing.

They decided to go upstairs. As Phoebe's hand brushed the banister, a sudden feeling of disquiet and alarm surged through her. A startling long-forgotten memory assaulted her senses. For an instant she was a child again, playing at a neighbor's house. The neighbor had a beautiful golden retriever named Bear. When the neighbor's father came home, Bear leaped up on him, licking his face. No dog ever loved his master more than this one. When the man sat on the couch to read his paper, Bear leaped up next to him and planted his snout on the man's belly and worked his muzzle back and forth as he moaned and let out a low, mournful despairing sound that his owner said was "purring."

It didn't sound like puppy purring to Phoebe.

The animal repeated the behavior every chance it had. It became a running joke in the house until one night, when the man ran into his physician at the local movie theater. The doctor was not amused. He looked gravely at the man and ordered him to show up at the office first thing in the morning.

There had been a malignancy that might have killed him if it had gone undiagnosed much longer. Bear's unnaturally acute sensitivities had saved his master's life.

The memory faded. Phoebe gasped and quickly drew her hand away from the banister. Perhaps because of her time as an empath, she was sensitive to the house's feelings, its strength and vitality, and now to a weakness lingering at its core. A sickness, something dark that might eat the house away from within, destroying it.

What she had just felt wasn't the ghost. Phoebe was certain of that much. The wraith they had encountered had been gleeful and filled with light and exuberance. There'd been nothing dark about him.

"There *is* something else here," Phoebe whispered.

And somehow, she was going to find it.

A few moments later, Phoebe was on the third floor. She heard heavy breathing from behind a rattling door, as if someone was holding the knob closed with two shaking hands. Phoebe knocked on the door and called out.

"Phoebes?" came Piper's strangled cry. "Is it gone?"

"Is what gone?" Phoebe asked.

The door whipped open. Piper jammed her pale face out, looked around, and breathed a sigh of relief. "It couldn't fit through the door," Piper explained absently. "I should have figured that out sooner."

Phoebe stroked her sister's back. "What are you talking about?"

Piper frowned, as if embarrassed to say. But as the sisters left that door behind, Phoebe noticed something that had escaped her before.

Deep ragged clawlike grooves had been carved into the door. Clawlike? But that was ridiculous, of course. Anything that could leave claw marks that big would have a heck of a time even fitting in the corridor!

Phoebe and Piper found Paige and all the others in the study, where music blared, bodies danced, and a shining supernatural chandelier was spinning wildly above their heads. Dazzling crystal shards struck off from the chandelier, sailing through the air and piercing the bodies of the wildly swaying dancers. When it happened, the dancer that was struck shuddered and shrieked with laughter and delight—and danced even faster.

"It's like a caffeine cacophony," Karl said, his back pressed up against some bookcases. "As if these people needed to be even more wired."

"No, it feels great," yelled Jessica as she leaped into the fray.

"This place is magic," called Cassie.

"Anyone come up with any clues on the ghost-hunting front?" called Piper. She was met with a chorus of "later, later" and distracted waves. So much for "meeting back in two hours to compare ghost-hunting notes." All these folks wanted to do was have fun.

Kevin was dancing with Paige, but his gaze continually flickered to Cassie and Ryan. Craig was bumping and grinding all by himself, while Tamara made a show of looking like she didn't care while the edge of her vision was planted on his backside.

Phoebe looked to Karl and thought, *Well, if I were a darksome demony type, I'd for sure latch on to this guy. Who'd be able to tell the difference in his behavior after he was possessed?*

"So, how do you know Kevin?" Phoebe asked casually.

Karl shrugged. "We went to school together. The legend, as he tells it, is that I was the first person to read his work and tell him that it had real worth. Of course, coming from me, that meant I thought he could earn a small fortune off it at some point, which"—he looked around and gestured smugly at the vastness of the mansion surrounding them—"I'd say it was a pretty solid call. He has a very vivid imagination."

Well, Karl's a creep, that's for sure, Phoebe decided. *But a demon? Hard to say . . .*

Jessica eased back as Craig walked by, sighing as she took in the view. She wasn't the only one. Paige and Craig were exchanging very knowing glances.

The breathtaking and reportedly harmless streaks of light crept closer, and Phoebe backed away from the brilliant shards of rainbow illuminating the room. Something about the lovely gleaming streaks of brilliance disturbed her in ways she couldn't put into words.

Suddenly, something warm and furry scampered against the back of her ankle. She turned, twisted, and yelped in surprise. A tiny black form burst into view, then disappeared behind the couch.

A cat? Phoebe thought, remembering the gigantic grooves in the door upstairs. *What—*

Then she was falling, slamming against the bookshelves, her hand reaching out for anything that might right her, but all she did was haul a stack of books down with her as she smashed to the floor. Piper and Paige were at her side in a moment.

Paige examined her ankle, which Phoebe seemed to have twisted on the way down, and said, "She's fine."

Piper's attention was firmly fixed on a book

that had fallen in Phoebe's lap. Peeking out from between its bindings was a collection of notepad pages that might have been torn from a diary or journal. After the sisters had extricated themselves from the attention of the other well-meaning partygoers, who were now contenting themselves with a new series of ghostly goings-on, Phoebe examined the loose pages, her lips pursing in surprise.

"Well, that's interesting," Phoebe declared. "It's a diary from a guy named Gino, who worked for Robert Maxwell. It describes the night he disappeared, and in pretty good detail too. The really strange thing is, what would those pages be doing here, hidden away like that?"

"Didn't you say that more than one writer stayed here, planning to write the 'true story' of what happened to Maxwell and the later hauntings?" asked Paige. "Maybe one of the writer guys bought this Gino dude's journal, hid the pages here, then had to take off in a hurry for some reason and never got to come back for them."

Piper raised an eyebrow in alarm. "Or maybe this writer guy *couldn't*. We only *think* no one's been hurt in the house. Maybe we don't know the full story either."

"Well, there's one person I'd really like to talk to," Phoebe said, referring to the strange young woman who had come in the guise of a singing-telegram girl. She had cast what could only have been a truly momentous spell binding the actor into the house. "Her name was Emily. Maybe she had a daughter or granddaughter who could help us."

Piper nodded. "If we understood why this witch took his life and cursed him—"

Paige ran her hand through her lustrous hair. "No, it wasn't a curse. The way she was acting? She was into this guy!"

Phoebe agreed. "Yeah, and Maxwell didn't die—he disappeared!"

"Do the math," Piper urged. "These clippings say he was forty-two when he disappeared, and that was in nineteen twenty-six—Eighty years ago. That would make him 122 if he were still around. And unless he was a demon or something . . ."

"Gotcha, he'd be a goner by now for sure!" Phoebe said. Her brow furrowed in concentration. "The gardener says he saw weird lights when the woman was giving Maxwell that singing telegram, and then he just disappeared. It's possible that she... what's the word . . . consigned his soul to the house."

"Like what you'd do with an old dress?" asked Paige.

Phoebe raised an eyebrow. "No! I mean, yeah, kinda. Maybe she bound him to the house."

Paige set her hands on her hips. "But that would make her . . . a good witch!"

"Bingo," Piper declared. "And *that* means she just might still be around herself. Time to do some checking."

"But how?" asked Phoebe.

Piper smiled. "How else?" She cleared her throat. "Leo!"

Chapter 7

The blazing sun beat down on the streets of Los Angeles as the Charmed Ones pulled up before a bright shining silver box of a seven-story building. Leo had worked through the night to locate any trace of the witch who had zapped Maxwell into his current ghostly calling, and this was where his investigations had led the witches.

The building had been rendered in the classic Bauhaus design popular in the 1920s. Inside and out, the building sported straight edges and smooth, slim forms. Even the furniture in the spacious lobby had been crafted from sleek, shining steel.

Piper found an intercom button and leaned on it for the seventh-story loft. After a moment, a bright chipper voice answered.

"Yello!"

"Emily DuChancey?" Piper asked.

The intercom crackled. "Yes . . ."

With a snarky edge in her voice, Piper asked, "Still delivering singing telegrams?"

A moment of silence shot from the speaker, then the woman on the other end said, "Pardon. I think you must—whoa, Nellie! I can actually *feel* your power from here. No point in denying it, I guess." She suddenly broke into a silly singsong. *"You're all witchies, I'm a witchie, wouldn't-cha like to be a witchie too?"* She hit the buzzer, and the door unlocked. "Come on up, sisters."

The trio regarded one another as they entered and climbed the stairs.

Paige shuddered. "That voice. Her singing . . ."

"I know," Piper said, her teeth still gritted. "There's tone-deaf, then hearing something like that and wishing you were tone-deaf!"

"Not to be mean or anything," Phoebe added, "but I kinda see why the whole music career thing never took off for her."

The woman who opened the door for them looked eighteen—maybe. Her red plaid micro-mini swirled over torn jeans and gleaming black boots while a tight white crop top completed the look. A pair of silver serpent bands adorned her upper arms, and her blond hair was swept into an old-fashioned pageboy do.

"What—am I on fire or something?" she asked, fending off the frantic stares the Charmed Ones awarded her.

Phoebe frowned. "No, we're looking for . . . your great-grandmother or—"

"It's me," Emily the witch said. "I just don't look my age."

Paige shook her head as they were shown into the living room and invited to plop down into the welcoming confines of an inviting, comfy couch. A handful of framed Robert Maxwell movie posters lined the walls. They were definitely in the right place!

"Youth spells?" Piper ventured. "Magic for personal gain? How did you escape the whammy that normally comes with that?"

"I didn't," Emily said, her voice choked with emotion. "The youth spell *was* the whammy."

Paige did a double-take. "Whoa, hold on. Eternal youth and beauty—this is a bad thing how, exactly?"

Emily eyes darkened. "I'll tell you the whole story, but, honestly there's not that much to it. I—"

"Waitaminute!" Piper cried, looking to a huge archway leading to the kitchen. "What's that I'm smelling?"

Phoebe shrugged. "Um . . . cherry pie?"

Springing to her feet, Piper raced to the kitchen. Emily watched her with a bemused smile.

"What is it, what, what?" demanded Phoebe as she attempted to spring from the supernaturally soft couch cushions. It wasn't easy. "Is she cooking up some potion that'll bring doom and destruction to Innocents?"

"Smells magically delicious to me," Paige offered, gently easing her way off the couch, then bounding to her feet. "Or is that something else?"

They burst into the enormous kitchen, the stunned Piper stumbling in circles, staring at dozens of pies waiting to be placed in ornately designed boxes and shipping crates.

"*You're* Grandma Em?" Piper cried incredulously as Emily swept in behind them. "Of Grandma Em's Holistic Whole Pies and Treats?"

"That would be me," Emily proudly proclaimed.

Sadness struck Piper's pretty face. "Tell me you're *not* using magic in these."

Emily laughed. "I'm not. These *are* just like my gramma used to make," Emily assured them. "I was born in 1906. I learned to bake from scratch, all natural ingredients. I just do it the old-fashioned way—and then sell on the Internet. I may have been around for a century, but I'm still a modern girl."

"Wow," Paige said, leaning back against a cupboard. "I've got to admit, you're nothing like what I would have expected."

"You know what they say," Emily mused. "Adapt or . . . or feel real out of place and bored 'cause you have no idea what everybody else is talking about."

They settled in the living room, each with a slice of homemade pie. Emily sauntered into the kitchen to check on a couple of pies.

"Well, no cats, at least," Paige muttered. "Can't explain why, but if there were cats, too, I'd find this downright creepy. Hundred-year-old witch sitting us down with pie and a story. Add in some cats? I'd be out of here. It'd just be too much."

Emily breezed back in.

"*Good* pie." Paige exclaimed.

Phoebe nodded. "*Great* pie."

"So," Piper said. "I think you know why we're here."

"Well, you're the Charmed Ones," Emily said. "I can tell that from your auras."

"You don't seem all that surprised to see us," ventured Piper.

Emily leaned back and stretched. "I always knew it would be just a matter of time before I got that knock at the door. Honestly, it's kind of a relief."

Piper set down her pie, her expression suddenly turning hard. "So why'd you do it? Why'd you kill Robert Maxwell?"

"Slow down, sister!" Emily cried, bolting upright in her love seat. "I never killed anyone. I'd never use magic like that. What do you take me for?"

"I'm not sure," Piper said. "But we've just seen Maxwell's ghost, so unless the rules of the universe have changed and no one let me know, I'm kinda thinking he was breathing before you got to him and wasn't when you were through."

Emily settled back in her easy chair. "True. I rendered him, body and spirit, into the house."

"He's *still* alive?" Paige asked through a heapin' mouthful of pie.

Emily rolled her eyes. "Come on now, girls. With everything you've seen, everything you've been through as the Charmed Ones, you've got to have an idea by now of exactly how limiting concepts like life and death truly are, right? I took him beyond the reach of concerns like that and gave him what he truly wanted."

Piper couldn't believe what she was hearing. "He *asked* you to make him a haunting spirit?"

"No!" Emily said. "Not in so many words . . . Listen, have you ever been in love? I mean, head-over-heels in love, out of your mind in love, light-years past making any kind of sense or listening to the people whose opinions mean the most to you in love? In love with—and this is the best part—someone who doesn't even know you're alive?"

"Oh, yeah," Piper said snidely. "Nowadays we have a word for that. Stalker."

Emily laughed and kicked her legs like a little girl. "Uh-huh, pretty much! Except"—her expression suddenly became deathly serious— "except *no*, not really, not even a little. I was off my head, but I knew what I was doing."

Paige leaned forward. "Just to be clear, we're

talking about your fixation on Robert Maxwell, the actor, in nineteen twenty-six."

"Spot on, sweetie," Emily said softly. "You're actually a lot smarter than you look!"

Paige looked up from her pie. "Thanks! I . . . think."

"I just mean . . ." Emily shrugged. "Well, look at me. Everyone writes me off as some kind of ditz. Truth is, I've received three medical degrees to date and I was part of the essential research team that discovered the best way to treat ailments stemming from the blood-brain barrier deterioration." She laughed to herself. "I also run a fansite for Brad Pitt and I've been in five low-budget horror flicks so far. Everyone says I've got this great scream. Wanna hear it?"

Piper tensed. "Uh, no, really, that's—"

Emily threw her head back and loosed the most ear-piercing scream any of the Charmed Ones had ever heard. Even demons writhing in the agony of going up in flames as they were vanquished didn't sound like *that*.

"*And* you bake pies," Piper put in.

"I do," Emily said seriously. "And people love them. I ship all over the world. Can't even come close to keeping up with the demand. But I'm not gonna franchise—that would ruin the whole thing."

"So . . . Maxwell. You were in love with him," prompted Paige, desperately attempting to keep this wacky witch on track.

"Oh, right. Yeah, I'm a little scattered, I admit it. . . ." She drew a sharp breath. "Focus, focus . . . here we go. Robert Maxwell was dying. Only a handful of people knew it. I'll spare you the technical babble and just say that what was wrong with him had to do with his brain, and he didn't have long. He felt fine the night of the premiere, but that wasn't going to last. All he knew was that something was wrong. Fainting spells, some motor-coordination issues, a lot of other symptoms that could just be written off on account of too many margaritas and too much partying, even back then. He thought he needed to just slow down, clean up his act, get spiritual, and that would take care of everything. He had this big retreat to Tibet planned and everything. His doctor hadn't told him the truth yet. Doc Phillips was waiting until after Robert's big movie opened. In fact, I was supposed to call him the next day and ask him to come in. . . ."

"You worked for his doctor?" asked Piper.

"I was the receptionist," Emily explained. "Cute and perky, those were the two big requirements for the job. Robert was always kind of sad and uncomfortable when he came to the office. Like he was embarrassed by the fact that he was only human, that he could get a cough or catch the flu, that he wasn't really one of those perfect men he played on the big screen. I think he always felt a responsibility to his fans to be larger than life, to be something more, and—"

"And you got all this from what?" asked Piper quickly. "You never even talked to him, right?"

"I listened in when he was with the doc," Emily said, not taking offense. "I told you, I was in love, but I wasn't crazy. It's just . . . you could see it in his eyes. This fear he would try to hide from everyone, and for the most part succeeded. Except when he came to the office. He was like a big, sweet kid who thought, any minute now, this fantastic ride was going to come to an end, that people were going to find out that he really didn't know what he was doing and it was all going to be taken away. Everything he loved . . . and he didn't get it. He didn't understand that it wasn't about training, or anything like that. He just brought himself to every role, and he was a kind, decent man. A good man. And we all know how hard that is to find."

"Got that right," Phoebe murmured.

Emily drew a deep breath. "It was so sad, it broke my heart to see it, so . . . I made a decision. I had been to his mansion before, dropping off a gift from Doc Phillips. I knew what that place was, I sensed its power the same way I sensed yours."

"What do you mean?" asked Phoebe intently.

"It's like . . ." She rolled her eyes. "How to describe it . . . it's like a big battery with an off-the-scale psychic charge from all the crazy things that have happened within its walls over the centuries."

"Centuries?" asked Paige.

"Uh-huh," Emily answered. "It was originally built in England a very long time ago, then moved here, stone by stone. It's enchanted. I went to his place, I cast my spell, and I made Robert Maxwell and that house one and the same. So long as it stands, he will be there with it. And I've been making the most of the life that's been left to me after the personal gain whammy ever since."

"You thought you were doing him a favor," Paige said softly. "Sparing him from the truth of what was happening to him, preserving his place in Hollywood and giving him the chance to give performances . . . forever."

"That would about sum it up," Emily said cheerfully. "More pie, anyone?"

"And your punishment for using magic for selfish ends has been immortality," Piper said, disregarding the generous offer, even though her tummy cursed her for it. Those pies were amazing! "Doesn't exactly sound fair."

Emily sighed. "Well, look at it this way. Immortality's fun, for a while. But when you don't age, and everyone around you does, then it starts being not so fun. Having to rebuild your life and take on a new identity every ten years or so is a major drag. And Maxwell . . . I can't even see him. It's part of the whammy. I can't go into the house, I can't get anywhere near it, not unless he invites me, and he doesn't know he needs to."

"You could try sending him a singing telegram," Piper suggested.

"I've considered it," Emily said. "I guess . . . I'm just scared. Even after all these years, I'm terrified that he doesn't understand what I did for him and why. What if he hates me?"

Even Phoebe didn't know what to say to that, not at first. Then, finally, she said, "We could ask him for you."

Emily's eyes widened with hope and fear. "You'd do that for me?"

"For a lifetime supply of pie," Piper suggested, forlornly eyeing her plate. "Just kidding!"

"Is there any way to reverse the spell?" asked Paige. "To set him free, that is."

Easing back, Emily admitted, "Okay, here's the deal. I've thought about it, but for some reason, maybe 'cause of the whammy, I can't remember the exact wording I used. Without that . . ."

"Without that, it's impossible," Phoebe added. "But I bet Maxwell remembers!"

"I'm sure he does," Emily said. "But from everything I've heard over the years, you're going to run into one big problem: He *loves* haunting that house. I don't see him telling you the spell in a million years."

Chapter 8

The Charmed Ones stopped at the apple grove before continuing on to the mansion. They didn't want the house, or Maxwell, overhearing the tail end of their conversation.

Paige picked a nice, ripe apple and settled back against a heavy comforting tree trunk as she swung her legs over a branch a dozen feet above her sisters, who stretched out on the grass below.

"The bottom line here is that without Maxwell's help, there's no way we can reverse the spell that's binding him to the house," Paige said, eyeing the perfect apple. "And look at things now. He's been waiting for eighty years for an audience that would appreciate him like this. You really think he's going to want to leave now?"

Piper stared up at the clouds. "What about Kevin? Do you think he'd really want to share his life with a spirit?"

"There's only one way to find out," Paige said. "I'll ask him."

"I still think there's something else here," Phoebe added, lazily brushing at the grass. The house has power, and Maxwell's real—he's a part of it, I accept that. But power can be a heck of a lure, especially to the dark, nasty types."

Piper sighed. "So why doesn't Maxwell ask for help?"

"Could be the typical guy thing," suggested Piper. "Leo *still* can't just ask for directions or for a hand opening a jar. Maxwell's old-school, he may be, like, 'I have to handle things myself, that's what guys do.'"

Paige pulled away from the apple she'd been chomping on. "No, that just doesn't track. He's helped people, he's saved people. If something dark and threatening was here, he'd try to warn people. I'm sure of it."

"So maybe there isn't anything," ventured Piper.

Phoebe frowned. "I know what I felt. I know what my senses were telling me."

Paige climbed down and tumbled gently toward her sister. "It could be that you don't. You're not an empath anymore. The house might just be messing with you, trying to throw you off Maxwell's trail."

"So there's really nothing else we can do about Maxwell?" asked Phoebe.

"We could trap him and try to take him out of

the house," Piper said flatly. "Or siphon the house's power. Other than that, I'm not sure."

"I don't know if we should even be considering that," Phoebe said. "So far, no one's been hurt."

"I think we should be playing matchmaker," Paige said. "Get Maxwell and Emily together."

"You're assuming that would get Maxwell out of the house," Piper said. "I'll hand it to Emily: She looks awesome and makes some mean pies, but no matter what she says, she's a little wacky. For all we know, she might want to join him here in the house."

The trio rose and started for the house.

"Yeah, well, we've got a bigger problem with Ryan and Karl," Paige reminded them. She had filled her sisters in on what she and Craig had overheard the previous night. "Cassie's got to know what a creep Ryan really is, that he's just using her."

"And that he's got it in for Kevin," added Phoebe.

They heard blaring music even before they went inside the manor. Yet again, the gang was partying.

In the dining room, Kevin, Cassie, and Tamara were giggling hysterically—and covered in fudge. Ryan sat in a corner, watching them, hiding his glare behind a pair of mirrored sunglasses. He forced a tolerant smile into place.

"I can't believe the way the kitchen just blew up!" Cassie squealed.

Kevin laughed. "I know! But it wasn't really hot or anything either, just medium warm so it would be good and gooey, didn't hurt at all."

"Wanna mud-wrestle?" asked Cassie.

"You mean fudge wrestle," Kevin replied, laughing so hard, he nearly fell over. Cassie clung to him, and their clothes happily slopped and sloshed together.

Running a finger along her soft, chewy-coated sleeve, Tamara tasted the fudge and nodded appreciatively. "Good stuff."

Paige parted with her sisters and found Craig.

"So," Paige said in a low conspiratorial hush as she leaned in close to Craig, "have you been keeping an eye on tweedle-dee and tweedle-dumber?"

"I have," he admitted, understanding that she meant Ryan and Karl. "And I see your sister Phoebe's back to keeping an eye on me. I think she's trying to figure out how all these weird special effects are happening. I have to admit, it kind of makes sense to look at the group of us. So far as we know, we're the only ones here."

Paige grinned. "Ya know, people keep seeing the two of us together, they might start to suspect that we're up to no good."

Craig leaned in close enough to smell her hair. He sighed. "That would be terrible. Maybe we should act like we're flirting. Divert attention from our actual secret agent duties."

"Maybe," Paige agreed, edging close enough to brush his nose with hers and giggle. Then, out of the corner of her eye, she saw Piper glance her way and mouth the words *"man-crazy."*

With a sudden scowl, Paige pulled away from Craig. "Any ghostly goings-on while we were gone?" she asked.

"Nothing to speak of," replied the confused Craig. "Did I do something wrong?"

"No," Paige said quickly. "It's not you."

Paige rejoined her sisters.

"So how do we make contact with Maxwell?" asked Piper. "Last time I tried, I got chased around by a two-ton cat for my trouble."

"I'm still not convinced that was Maxwell," Phoebe said. "Maybe the house was just trying to protect him from you."

"We need answers and we need 'em fast," Paige added. "This weekend will be over before you know it. Clock's ticking, and we've got two couples to try to get together before we go!"

And if there is *something wrong with the house, we need to find it and fix it*, thought Phoebe. *Before it's too late.*

Sparkling laughter filtered in through the glass double doors leading to the pool.

"The pool's incredible!" Jessica said, toweling herself off and not minding the attention her itsy-bitsy bikini was receiving from the male contingent of the guest roster. She looked to Cassie. "Sure you don't want to take a dip?"

Cassie looked away sheepishly and said, "Truth is, I can't swim."

"No way!" Jessica cried. "You're like Wonder Girl and the Power Twins put together."

Laughing, Cassie shrugged. "I'm scared of the water. Always have been. It may be why I'll run into burning buildings or jump out of planes. I'm compensating. That's what my therapist used to call it."

"Well, every superhero's got to have some kind of Kryptonite."

Paige watched them, sadness gripping her. Paige knew that she could just tell Cassie what she had overheard, but why should Cassie believe her? Paige had no proof, and even though what Paige would be telling her would be the absolute truth, it could so totally seem fabricated just to push Kevin and Cassie together. There had to be some other way of opening Cassie's eyes—but what?

Paige suddenly remembered the ghostly whisper at her neck warning her to take cover in the hall just before Ryan and Karl had appeared. Maxwell!

The ghost had cast Ryan in the role of a villain right off the bat, as if he'd just sensed Ryan's true nature. *Hmmm*, she thought. *How do you get an actor's attention?*

Inspiration struck Paige like a bolt from the blue. "You offer him a role."

She ran to Kevin's side.

"I think I've got it, and I'm going to need your help," Paige said. "Have your laptop with ya?"

"Sure," Kevin replied.

Paige grinned. "Good! Boot it up. We're going to make Robert Maxwell an offer he can't possibly refuse. . . ."

The rest of the afternoon and early evening was consumed by preparations. The "cast and crew" at Maxwell Manor were getting everything ready for their little show. Kevin worked hard on refining the script from the bare outlines of the plot that he and Paige had worked out, while the rest of the partygoers set to work on dressing the "sets" and getting into character. Everyone had a job to do, even Ryan and Karl, which was a good thing, as it left them no time to work on whatever scheme they might have been developing on their own.

Jessica's bedroom had a distinct Persian flavor in its decor, and the rest of the manor had been delightfully ransacked by the guests to turn the room into a full-blown Arabian harem. Jessica herself was outfitted in a gown fit for a princess—or a belly dancer. And Craig the crazy clown was typecast right into the part of the clueless, scimitar-wielding, bare-chested hero.

"You should be the one playing the princess in disguise," Jessica told Cassie, who, along with Paige, was handling her hair and makeup.

"Nah," Cassie said, anxiously casting her gaze to the balcony and the sprawling swimming pool beyond. Her heart suddenly thundered. "I wouldn't want to make Ryan any more jealous than I already have this weekend."

"He's the jealous type, huh?" Paige put in quickly. She was willing to seize on any opportunity to seed some discontent about the man who would soon propose to Cassie simply to further his position with his family.

Cassie's shoulders fell. "No, not really." Her gaze went to the pool again. "I was just using that as an excuse. I'm just too much of a scaredy-cat about falling into that pool to even think about being a part of this."

"Ah," Paige said, masking her disappointment.

"You really think this will work?" asked Jessica. "We put on a show with one part uncast, and at the right moment, the ghost will appear in that role?"

"I've already seen the script pages we left lying around, moving by themselves!" Paige said. "I think he's already working on his character."

Downstairs, Phoebe swung close enough to Kevin and Karl to overhear their friendly bantering as they readied a handful of props that would be needed during the "rescue" portion of the scene.

"So," Karl said urgently, "are you going to

share your special-effects wizardry with us now or keep us guessing?"

"It's got nothing to do with me," Kevin said honestly. "The ghost makes the rules, we just play by 'em."

Karl sighed. "If only I could figure out where you're keeping all your worker bees. You must have a dozen assistants running around behind the scenes setting things up, but I haven't seen or heard a thing."

"More things in heaven and earth?" ventured Kevin, casually referencing the famous line from Shakespeare's *Hamlet*.

"I don't think so," countered Karl. "Not in my philosophy."

"You might want to think about changing philosophies there, pal," Phoebe muttered.

"Excuse me?" Karl said with his customary air of distaste.

"Nothing," Phoebe sang happily as she worked on the props. "Nothing at all . . ."

Outside, by the pool, Piper was surveying the spot where the ghostly Maxwell would make his entrance, provided all went according to plan. Ryan stood at the other end of the pool, gazing deeply into the gently swaying water with a darkly satisfied expression that sent chills down Piper's spine. Something about his manner signaled to Piper that he was up to no good. But what exactly was he planning?

She fought the temptation to freeze him where he stood.

Night fell, and with it came the exciting murmuring throughout the house as "showtime" neared! Paige could practically feel the ghost's giddiness at what was to come. She rushed upstairs to Jessica's bedroom and burst in to find Cassie there alone.

"Where's Jess?" Paige asked.

"I don't know!" Cassie cried, checking her watch. "It's just about time and I haven't seen her or Craig."

A low rumble of dissatisfaction escaped Paige as she pictured Jessica getting her claws into the handsome comedian—and forgetting all about the show.

"I'll go find them," Paige promised. "You want to come with?"

"No," Cassie told her. "Ryan said that Kevin wanted to meet me up here just before we got started. Last-minute fittings and detail stuff. You know Kev."

Paige laughed. "Yup!"

The auburn-haired witch hesitated at the door, looking back at Cassie sitting on the edge of the huge bed. Paige was suddenly gripped by a feeling of sadness and dread.

"What is it?" Cassie asked.

Paige nearly blurted everything out right then and there. "Nothing," Paige said, plastering a smile into place. "Not a thing."

Cassie was left with an odd feeling after Paige left and shut the door on her way out. Cassie wandered to the window, her legs turning to lead as she approached the balcony and the view of the swimming pool below. She hugged herself, rubbing at her bare arms as a sudden chill struck her. It felt a lot like the cold spot she'd experienced in the hall, and she darted forward to avoid it.

There it was again!

She drove forward, to the balcony, and the sensation chased her there, manifesting whenever she paused and thought herself safe.

"This isn't funny," she growled low and deep in her throat.

"Actually, my dear, that depends entirely upon your point of view," whispered a dark echoing voice at her back. She whirled—but no one was there.

"Kevin?" Cassie called, turning from the balcony and wringing her hands. She suddenly smelled smoke. Racing to the single door leading in or out of the vast bedroom, Cassie saw smoke filtering in from the crack under the door.

There was a fire!

Cassie's hands shot up, palms open, and she pressed them to the door. It was red-hot, and she knew exactly what that meant. Hungry flames were whirling and seeking on the other side of the door, and if she opened that door, they would rush in with an explosive gust and burn her alive.

Cassie backed away from the door, her gaze

darting frantically about the room. "Kevin? Kevin, listen to me, I need help!"

But the taunting voice had fallen silent. Only the cold spots remained. They burst into existence once more, driving Cassie toward the balcony—and an inescapable conclusion: She would have to leap from the balcony into the pool. It was the only way to save herself.

The room was already filling with smoke. Cassie began to cough and choke. In seconds, the fire would arrive and it would swallow this room whole, with her in it.

She edged her way to the balcony, the fresh night air a welcome relief. She didn't see any of her friends below; in fact, dark swirls seemed to whip about where she might have expected to see other party guests.

Cassie tried to call out, but the smoke leaped down her throat, searing her, making it impossible for her to speak.

I'll climb down, Cassie thought, her gaze fixed on the vines covering the balcony and the mansion walls. With a single trembling hand, she reached for them.

Below, near the door leading to the vast pool, Paige and Kevin nearly collided as they rushed together from opposite directions.

Nearly out of breath, Kevin asked, "Have you been able to find Jess or Craig?"

"No," replied Paige, feeling a little irked. "So . . . how did things go with Cassie?"

Kevin stared at her blankly. "What are you talking about?"

"Cassie told me that you two were going to meet up in Jessica's room to discuss some last-minute preparations."

"No," replied Kevin. "I've been searching for Craig and Jess. I haven't seen Cassie for a while."

"Oh, okay," Paige said, pulling away from her friend. "Guess I just misunderstood."

She went back to searching for the missing "actors" while fighting the feeling that something very strange was going on.

Forget it, she chided herself. *You just feel guilty because you haven't told Kevin about what Ryan and Karl were up to yesterday.*

Paige and Craig had talked about letting Kevin know that the pair were plotting against him, but neither was sure he'd be able to bring himself to believe it. Kevin's incredibly kind nature just didn't allow for such things. And if all went as planned tonight, all their plotting and planning wouldn't mean much, anyway.

Meanwhile, high above, Cassie eased herself over the balcony railing and gripped the vines tightly with both hands. She still couldn't see the partygoers below—nor could they see her. There was magic at work, powerful dark magic that had nothing to do with the house—except that it drew slightly on the house's great power—or the ghost of Robert Maxwell.

This magic was pure evil.

Cassie eased her lithe body into the darkness, nervously lowering one hand while keeping a firm grip with the other. *Don't look down*, she cautioned herself as she heard the gently lapping water below, *don't be afraid*.

As she moved lower on the vines her hand closed on something cold, wet, and slippery—and suddenly she lost her grip, her wet hand flying out into the night, her body wheeling over the pool. The vines just under the balcony rail had been recently greased, as if someone *knew* she would try to climb down this way.

Panicked, Cassie reached up with her slippery hand to the balcony's edge but couldn't reach it, her fingers slipping, sliding—then the vine, which she could now see had been cut partway through, suddenly snapped.

With a shrill scream she plunged toward the pool.

Paige and Kevin were just emerging from the dining room's double doors once again as Cassie's scream pierced the night. A heavy splash struck a dozen yards from the pair and they saw Cassie's wildly whipping arms, her kicking legs, her terror-struck face as her momentum dragged her down into the gigantic pool's deep end.

Kevin broke from Paige and leaped into the pool just as another splash sounded. Ryan had also dived in; he had been much closer to where

Cassie had fallen—and had already changed into swimwear. But these details escaped notice as the witnesses to the "accident" were only concerned with Cassie's welfare.

The swimmers surged to the spot where Cassie had disappeared, but before either had arced a dozen paces, the pool's surface suddenly twisted into a churning, turbulent whirlpool, whipping both men around in wide circles as a spiraling depression formed exactly where Cassie had floundered and gone under seconds earlier.

A giant hand struck out from the center of the whirlpool, a blue luminous hand the size of a Volkswagen that held the limp form of the waterlogged Cassie. The hand expanded down into an arm that burst from the water as a great blue bald head next sprung from the whirlpool. The bald blue head sported gleaming eyes the size of manhole covers, a hooked nose and a wicked grin, and long, dangling diamond earrings.

A three-story-high Arabian Djinn flew up from the pool, his crimson vest billowing, his lower half twisting away into smoke that filtered into a fine bed of mist that crawled along the surface of the pool. Shiny gold serpent bands wrapped around the muscular meat of his right upper arm while a trio of dangling gold bands clanked together at his opposing wrist, where Cassie lolled.

The Djinn gently laid Cassie onto the concrete at the edge of the pool as Ryan and Kevin scrambled from the churning water and raced to her. Ryan reached her first, and he gently held back her hair as she coughed up the water in her lungs. Karl appeared, right on cue, holding out a large towel. Ryan wrapped the towel tightly around Cassie and held her close as she quaked and shuddered. Kevin could do nothing but stand nearby and watch with relief.

"It's okay, it's all right," Ryan murmured. "I've got you now and I'll never let you go. You're safe, it's over."

Paige was shaken by what had happened, but the moment she had planned for had arrived, after a fashion, at least, and she wasn't about to let it go. She would tell the ghost about Emily, but first she would ask, *I'd like to know if you're a see-all, tell-all kinda ghost. Like, if you saw something in the hall yesterday that people should know about, could you thread up a projector and replay it for everyone right now?*

But Paige never had the chance. The giant smashed his fist into the water, causing a wave that splashed all who had gathered there.

"You think it's over, do you?" cried the enraged Djinn as smoke billowed from Jessica's room. "Well, think again. The manor is on fire!"

Suddenly, a pair of faces burst from the smoke-filled balcony. It was Craig and Jessica.

"No fire, just a mean honker of a smoke

machine set outside the door!" Craig called. "And some other gizmo hooked up to the door to make it seem hot as blazes."

"Which of you nimrods locked us in that closet?" Jessica demanded.

A third form appeared behind them. Tamara belted the smoke from her face and stared down at her suit in despair. "Someone's getting a dry-cleaning bill for this. And it's a good thing I found these two, I—yikes!"

The trio on the balcony finally noticed the gigantic Djinn, whose eyes blazed with supernatural fury.

Paige stared in horror at the Djinn. He bellowed in fury, his features shimmering and shifting, as if some other force was tearing at him, sinking its hooks deeply into him, trying to control him like a puppet on a string.

"No, no," he muttered, "I've just saved the girl, now I should be basking in applause while staying sternly in character. Who . . . what . . . no, I couldn't, I mustn't—"

The giant whipped his hand back, and a thousand serpents suddenly materialized in his palm. He looked like a pitcher winding his hand back for a pitch, and the ball in this case would be hissing and deadly. And it was aimed at Kevin, Cassie, Ryan, and Karl.

Piper's hands flew up, and she froze the entire scene.

"Get them out of the way, fast!" Piper hollered.

Paige and Phoebe didn't need to be told twice. They rushed over to the frozen foursome.

Only—Kevin was stuck fast. Phoebe hauled Cassie away and was returning for Karl, even though she thought he was just a snake in human form and deserved whatever the Djinn was throwing, when she saw her half sister's distress. Paige dragged at Kevin's still body, but he might as well have been a stone statue. He wasn't going anywhere.

And above, the Djinn was shaking, quaking, somehow struggling to free itself of the effects of Piper's magic!

Phoebe dragged Ryan away, but before she could go back to grab Paige, the effects of Piper's spell were suddenly reversed and the Djinn hurled its honkin' fistful of snakes!

"Paige?" Kevin said, his brow knitted in confusion. Then he saw the flying serpents streaking right for the two of them and he was stunned into silence.

Paige knew that all eyes were on her, but she had to use her magic, she had no choice! A white sea of shimmering energy formed around her as she orbed Kevin and herself from the path of danger.

The ghost made me disappear before, why not? Paige thought.

She rematerialized at her sister's side, Kevin beside her—but he was only there for a heartbeat. He vanished again, yanked back in a blink to his original place by the pool, where he yelped as the incoming flight of snakes suddenly transformed into a sailing sea of scimitars!

"Defiler of my house!" hollered the fiery eyed Djinn. "Infidel!"

The scimitars struck, smacking hard into the concrete all around Kevin, only a handful streaking close enough to slice through his sleeves, part his hair, or leave light scratches on his arms and face.

The Charmed Ones readied themselves for another ghostly onslaught, but instead, the giant teetered and clutched wildly at his face, his features turning to mist. "No, no, I . . . I'd just as soon have tea and cakes with these nice people. . . . No, I don't care what it says in the script, I won't—I won't!"

With that, the Djinn vanished.

Ryan sprang to his feet and slammed Kevin back with a pair of open palms. "What were you thinking?" Ryan roared.

Kevin was stunned, unable to reply.

"Your little fun and games went too far this time," Ryan said. "Cassie could have been hurt, or worse. And those swords . . . I was supposed to be on the receiving end of them, wasn't I?"

"Now wait just a minute!" Paige called, stalking at the enraged man.

Ryan lunged at Kevin again, but Karl caught him and held him back.

"Thanks," murmured the startled Kevin.

"Don't thank me," Karl said. "I know exactly what was going on here. I do now, anyway. I should have put it together a lot more quickly."

Once the flaring tempers were somewhat under control, Karl explained step by step exactly how the "fire gag" had been achieved. He freely admitted his part in accepting delivery of the devices needed to pull it off along with all the other supplies that had been ordered for the evening's little play. But he laid responsibility for all of it onto Kevin, claiming he was only acquiring items Kevin asked for.

"That's not true," Kevin whispered.

Paige took his hand. "Don't worry, we'll get to the bottom of this."

Karl told the rest of his story, laying out every detail nice and neat as Craig, Tamara, and Jessica joined them. Cassie listened intently, her gaze fixed on Kevin the entire time.

"I took delivery for all this stuff that you ordered," Karl said, "but I had no idea what you were planning. You even locked Craig and Jess away. It's crazy. I guess you were planning to be the knight in shining armor for Cassie, to rescue her and finally make her see you the way you wanted her to. Or maybe you just wanted to make her hurt the way she hurt you. . . ."

"None of that's true!" Paige cried. "Craig and I overheard Ryan and Karl yesterday. They were—"

"Oh, and you just thought to mention this

now?" Karl said, cutting her off. "Kevin's ex to the rescue."

"It's not like that," Paige said, her face flushed.

"Kevin?" Cassie said in a small, disbelieving voice. Everyone fell silent as she strode forward.

"You thought that was funny or something? I could have been killed!" Cassie roared into Kevin's face. "You know I'm terrified of the water. How could you do that to me? I thought we were friends, I thought, maybe, that you even . . ." She shuddered, half turned away.

Ryan put his arm around Cassie and said, "Let's get out of here."

Cassie looked around bitterly, then her gaze locked with Kevin's. "Yes, let's."

"When we're alone," Ryan said softly, "there's something I want to ask you. . . ."

Ryan and Tamara took Cassie back to her room.

Paige shuddered. She had a very good idea what Ryan was going to ask Cassie. *He's going to propose to her now, while she's confused, angry, and vulnerable. I won't be surprised if she accepts.*

Karl leaned in close to Kevin and told him, "We're leaving tonight. What I'd like you to consider is this: We are totally within our rights to sue you for everything you've got, but I'll make a deal with you. Share the secrets of your special-effects tech with me, and I'll make sure all this goes away."

"I can't . . . ," Kevin said, his thoughts still swimming with the chaos of all that had happened.

"I think you will," Karl told him. "If you're smart."

Paige looked around, desperately hoping Maxwell would reappear and help. He seemed to know all and see all in this house. Why wasn't he doing something?

Soon, the Charmed Ones had gathered in the study while Craig and Jessica did their best to console the crushed Kevin.

"What have we done?" Phoebe asked.

"I know exactly what we did," Paige said. "We gave Ryan and Karl the perfect opportunity to set Kevin up. I was so busy thinking Maxwell would come swooping in to the rescue and make everything right that I never stopped to consider the opening Ryan and Karl would have."

"Maybe Maxwell has his own problems," Phoebe ventured. "He really didn't seem like himself there near the end. In fact, he looked pretty shook up."

"We can't blame ourselves for what Ryan and Karl did. If it hadn't been this, they would have come up with something," Piper assured her. "Maybe something a whole lot worse."

"I've got to talk to Cassie," Paige said. "I've got to try to get her to understand what really happened!"

"She won't see you," Phoebe said. "She won't see anyone except Ryan and those other two. And even if she did, she'd never believe anything you had to say."

"What about the ghost?" asked Paige. "What about Maxwell? Something was really wrong with him tonight. I couldn't believe the way he went after Kevin!"

"I'm with you there," Piper snarled savagely. "Those were *not* the actions of a friendly ghost."

Phoebe hugged herself. "I gotta say, I agree. We've got to deal with him."

"You mean like trap him, vanquish him?" Paige asked, aghast. "I'm sorry, I know what happened, but I just can't bring myself to believe that after all these years, Robert Maxwell went to the dark side. Maybe he's a method actor and he just got caught up in his role. This is probably the best audience he's had in years!"

Piper shook her head. "We have to make sure no one else gets hurt."

"I say we give the ghost a good talking-to and leave it at that," Paige insisted. But she looked away, worried. She could tell from the look in her sisters' eyes that they had something else in mind for the spirit.

Robert Maxwell was curled up alone in his dressing room, his knees under his jaw, quaking with disbelief. The small room was a secret chamber below the house that he had transformed and filled with costumes and props from many of his greatest performances. In all of his years as a haunting spirit, nothing like this had ever happened to him before.

"Spike, you know me," he said, peering into the darkened eye sockets of the skull that had been with him since his first performance of *Hamlet* in the Royal Shakespeare Company in '21, when he was visiting England. Now the skull was his only friend and confidant, though it never actually talked back. "I would never hurt *anyone*. In all these years—all these bravura performances, if I do say so myself—I've never come close to harming any living creature. But tonight . . . tonight, I wished to do great harm to an innocent guest of my happy home. I almost . . . I could have . . . I don't understand how it could have happened."

Suddenly, a darksome shape flickered in the actor's great ornate mirror. Someone was behind him!

Maxwell gasped and spun. In all his years, no one had ever intruded upon him here. How could they? He had walled the chamber up from every direction. No one could get in here, unless they could walk through walls.

Maxwell could see no one. Then, suddenly, a nightmare black figure melted into the shadows cast by the chamber's single flickering candle.

"You there!" the actor called. "Hello?"

But there was nothing and no one there, just unremitting darkness.

With a breathless sigh, the actor sank back into his makeup chair. "I must be going mad. I could have *sworn* someone was watching me. But no one is there. . . ."

Maxwell buried his face in his hands, unaware that the darkness behind him was once again on the move.

No, not the darkness. A thing that resided there.

A thing that plotted and planned with a malevolent will that would soon be felt by all within Maxwell Manor.

The thing had not been in the house long. But during its short stay, it had been watching, learning the rhythms of the house, gauging the vast reserve of power the house held and testing its ability to use that power. . . . Tonight, it had moved one step closer to achieving its goal by flexing its muscles and taking command of the ghost that had been grafted into the house's secret heart.

The writhing darkness considered consuming the foolish spirit. Keeping still was nearly impossible for the darksome, malevolent mass. It brimmed with destructive urges and ever-growing power that it leached from the great house.

Patience, it reminded itself. *All good things to those who wait. . . .*

Finally, Maxwell set down the skull and huddled in the corner, his eyes squeezed tightly shut.

Feeling perversely playful, the living dark-ness snatched up the skull and left the chamber. Skull in hand, the darkness surveyed the house, feeling its pulse, its rhythms. It held the skull high.

"Spike," said the darkness, "can you tell me how this mansion, this battery of vast power, evaded the notice of the Underworld and its seething legions of demons for so long? It was well-warded, of course, happily disguised as a mere curiosity on the mortal plane. But the spells and hexes surrounding the house only sheltered its true nature; they did not keep demons like myself from entering or taking the house's power."

The skull was silent.

The darkness laughed. "I see. You're loyal to your master. Well, have no fear, I will return you to him before he even notices that you are gone. But I must share my current victory with some-one, and you are the least likely to blab my plans to anyone. You see, the incident with your ghostly friend was a test. I could sense that Maxwell had been drawing upon the house's power for upward of eighty years, and I believed that he would present a formidable challenge to my plans. So I tested this great ghost—and my own power—in one fell swoop. Do you know what I learned?"

Spike stared at the darkness with hollow eyes.

"I learned that Maxwell is nothing," boasted the darkness. "I could dispel him with the simplest of incantations. But I won't do that . . . not yet, anyway. Maxwell still serves a purpose, so far as I'm concerned. And my own power and control over the house is growing greater with each passing moment. No, your ghostly master will pose no threat, and perhaps might still be put to use in some manner."

The darkness adjusted its grip on the skull, and Spike's lower jaw dropped open in alarm.

"Ah, yes, thank you for reminding me," the darkness chortled. "Your distress over my well-being could only stem from your knowledge that the Charmed Ones are here. Do not worry, I'm comfortable with letting the witches remain occupied with the playful ghost and all their purely human concerns as I gather greater reserves of power and fully ready myself to play my final hand. And of all the remaining mortals, the trio called Kevin, Cassie, and Ryan figure most heavily in my plans."

The darkness gestured, and a large screen appeared on the wall beside him. "Look, images, just like your master might make." Pictures formed on the screen, and the vacant skull looked out on a scene of Ryan and Karl plotting near the suit of armor.

"There is a coldness in Ryan's heart that delights me," admitted the watchful shadow-thing. "I will hardly need to give much of a performance at all when I take over Ryan's existence, using Ryan's notoriety, power, and position to further my own dark ends. Millions of people know intimate details about Ryan's existence. Men daydream about being him, women wish to be with him. And through those daydreams, I will find my way into the minds of so many ripe victims. . . ."

The darkness shuddered with delight. It looked at the skull, whose gaze seemed to be fixed on Cassie.

"Cassie will live," the shadow-thing assured the skull. It gestured, and a series of new images appeared on the "screen." The images were of Cassie and Ryan as a happily married couple jet-setting all over the world, waving to cameras, appearing before huge groups of people, and sitting at long tables, signing important papers.

"In my role as Ryan, I will give my new family anything and everything they desire, including this lovely bride," the darkness promised. "Ryan will become serious about their corporations, becoming more integral than ever before to their great workings throughout the globe, and that will give me an even greater stranglehold over the human world."

The images changed to pictures of Maxwell Manor.

"After Kevin's mysterious 'disappearance,' I will buy this house and return to it often for its mighty reserves of power," said the shadow creature. "Yes, with what I will take from two of them, I will achieve all of my wildest and darkest dreams. Once I have wealth and power, I will be able to pierce the minds of all humanity. I will enslave the mortal world and use the billions of creatures known as 'humans' as my army when I storm the gates of the Underworld and seize control."

The darkness spun the skull around, the images on the screen changing to visions out of a nightmare in which mindless human slaves fought legions of fiends in fiery pits. "Think of it. Imagine that you are just one of the helpless humans I will control. One night you will go to sleep and you will dream strange dreams of hellish dimensions and demonic masters. And when you wake, you will be a drone, a slave. You will be unable to say or do anything unless I wish it. And what I will wish is for you to learn the fine art of combat and slaying. Neighbors will rise against neighbors, you and your kind will murder one another in the streets, all so that I may identify those who will be fit to serve as proper warriors and weed out the rest. You will manufacture weapons, form armies, and when I say, you will go to hell and fight monsters in my name. Billions of humans will die, but what of it? Your sheer numbers are what I need to overwhelm the dark dimensions. And once I rule, I will transform the remnants of humankind into more demon slaves to help me rule the kingdoms I have conquered. . . ."

The darkness laughed in delight. It looked down at the skull—which was grinning.

"Oh," said the darkness glumly. "I see your point."

On the screen formed an image of Ryan and Cassie packing. Yes, a near calamity was at hand. Many of the humans, including Ryan and Cassie, were preparing to leave.

And that simply could not—would not—be allowed.

The darkness readied itself.

At quarter to nine that night, Kevin stood with the Charmed Ones at the base of the stairs in the main hall, waiting for Cassie and Ryan to come down on their way out of the house. Craig and Jessica were still racing about the house, desperately attempting to find some evidence that might refute Ryan and Karl's claims. Karl and Tamara had been glued to the side of the couple. It had been Tamara who had announced to all that Cassie and Ryan had indeed become newly engaged.

Tamara appeared at the top of the stairs.

"You should go," Tamara said stiffly as she eyed Kevin below. "Just let them leave in peace. Don't make this any harder than it needs to be."

"I didn't do any of it," Kevin said. "You have to believe me. If I could just see Cassie, just have a chance to explain . . ."

Paige's heart went out to her friend. Even

Tamara, the ice queen, seemed thawed by Kevin's distress. She descended the stairs slowly, wincing and grimacing as if she was fighting an inner battle against her own best instincts—and losing. Her logical side melted before Kevin's mute appeal.

Paige stepped forward. "It's true, you know. Kevin didn't have anything to do with what happened to Cassie."

Tamara waved a dismissive hand. "He wrote a script for the Arabian Nights scene. He was directing the whole production!"

"You know what I mean," Paige added firmly.

"For what it's worth," Tamara said softly, "I don't think Kevin would have done anything to intentionally hurt Cassie, not in a million years."

"It's Ryan and Karl, they set him up," Paige said urgently.

"Maybe," Tamara said wearily. "And if that's true, they did a great job of it, because while I don't think for a second that Kevin would have ever hurt Cassie on purpose, I do see him as shaken enough by losing Cassie to try just about anything to win her back. And it's not helping his case that he refuses to explain how all these crazy special-effects things have been engineered around the house."

"That's because he doesn't have anything to do with them," Paige insisted.

Tamara shrugged. "Then who does? The

ghost? You'll never get me to buy that. Cassie won't either."

Karl popped up from the head of the stairs. "Tamara, what did we discuss?"

The businesswoman adjusted her glasses and looked over her shoulder at Karl. "You don't give me orders. Remember that."

Sighing, Karl said, "This just makes things harder. If need be, I'll phone the police and bring them into this little matter."

"Maybe you should," Piper said fiercely. "I'm betting a good forensics team could dig up a whole lot of evidence that you and Ryan set Kevin up."

"I told you," Kevin interjected fiercely. "I don't want that. Cassie's been through enough."

"See?" asked Karl. "Spoken like a true guilty man."

"You're supposed to be Kevin's friend!" Phoebe shot at him.

Karl's snide laugh deflected the attempt to reach his "good side." "I don't think I ever really knew Kevin. It's hard to be friends with someone who could risk the life of the woman he supposedly loves. No, there's nothing between Kevin and me now."

Kevin nodded sadly. "Yeah, I'm getting that."

Karl turned at the sound of echoing footsteps. "That must be them. I'm asking the bunch of you one last time, clear out and let us leave without any more—"

His commandment was never completed. Instead, he paled at the sight of something other than the happy couple who suddenly lunged at him.

All Paige saw was a pair of smoky bands fly out and close on Karl. He shrieked, and the rings turned pure black and solidified like gigantic fingers that whipped back, hauling him out of view.

Tamara, who was standing on the steps, yelped as the stairs suddenly collapsed into a slide and she plunged down toward the startled witches. But before she could reach them, she slipped straight down through the floor and was gone.

Paige reached out to Kevin, but the wall behind him suddenly became fluid, the paneling flowing as it formed into a great gaping jagged tooth-filled mouth that chomped down on him, swallowing him whole with a single bite.

The Charmed Ones stared at one another in stunned silence for a single heartbeat, then, without a word, they bulleted into action. Paige grasped her sisters' hands and orbed them all to Cassie's bedroom, where giant spiders were hauling her to the ceiling by her hair while Ryan watched in disbelief. The giant cat that had terrorized Piper struck through the walls in an instant, snatching Ryan up in its fevered claws and spiriting him away.

They had been too late again.

Craig was in the conservatory when the Charmed Ones found him. The sculpture of the muses had come to life and grabbed him. The muses hauled him into the fountain and dragged him into its depths. When the witches reached the fountain, the surface had stilled and there was no trace of the statues—or Craig.

In moments, they found Jessica, the last of the Innocents, somehow drawn into the surface of the great mirror at the end of the corridor that had twisted around and around for them earlier. They watched as she vanished into its depths.

"Why weren't we taken?" Phoebe asked. "Everyone else . . . but not us."

"So much for your friendly ghost," said Piper.

Paige shook her head. "This isn't Maxwell."

They peered about, desperately attempting to come up with a plan, but everything had happened so quickly. . . .

Soon they were back in the dining hall, where the lights suddenly dimmed.

"It's a terrible thing, being powerless," said a low, booming voice that echoed all around the sisters. "Watching those you care about, or are sworn to protect, snatched away while you can do nothing to stop it."

An explosion of heat and light nearly lifted them from their feet. The Charmed Ones drew back as a familiar and terrifying form emerged from a cloud of fire rising before them. At first, it appeared to be made entirely of shadow, then it whipped the impenetrable cloak of darkness away and stood revealed in all its dark glory.

"I hadn't planned to tip my hand this early," said the demonic thing, "but you've given me no choice. I had to strike while my prey was still under one roof."

Phoebe gasped as she registered its emerald flesh, curling horns, and hooved feet. She knew this demon . . . she had helped destroy him.

"I note your confusion," the demon said with a hearty laugh. "I see you have not forgotten M'Gohrathet of the Clan Eesleviathan?" the demon asked.

"Demon of illusions from Chinatown," Phoebe said quietly. "Swore we'd pay big-time for vanquishing him. That guy?"

"He was my brother, and what he swore was true," the demon said. "I am X'ahroth, a fellow demon of illusion, and through me, he will have vengeance upon his destroyers!"

Piper scratched her head. "You mean, like, his instrument? A tool? You're just a big *tool*? I could have told you that!"

The demon roared in rage, not appreciating the joke. Windows exploded, and the sisters flew to the floor to avoid being sliced to ribbons.

"Have no fears," the demon said. "I have no wish to destroy any of you—yet. You must be made to pay in full for vanquishing my brother, and that will happen before this night is done. Then, my own agenda will begin. Until then, there will be games aplenty. Beginning with hide-and-seek. Find me, if you can, Charmed Ones. For time is already running out on the Innocents I have taken."

In a flash of flames, the demon vanished.

"Oh, poo," Piper breathed. "Paige, orb out of here, get Leo, a vanquishing potion, and whatever help you can get."

"On it," Paige said. Shimmering white light engulfed her, and her image flickered but did not fade. The light went away, and Paige was left rooted to the spot. "No can do, boss. Something's stopping me from orbing out of the house."

They checked their cell phones, which of course had no signal. The mansion's phones were also dead.

"Hmmm, one of us was convinced the ghost wasn't the real bad nasty around these parts," Phoebe said. "Not to say I told ya so, but . . . I told ya so."

"Fine, fine . . . ," muttered Piper.

"What we need to do is find the ghost," decided Paige. "We know he's not behind this. In fact, he's as much an innocent victim as everyone else."

"I don't see what we need him for," Piper said pragmatically. "He's just a cornball actor who likes to put on shows."

"Emily made him one with the house," Phoebe reminded her. "I've got some sensitivity to what's going on here, but it won't be anything like his. He should be able to tell us exactly where the demon is and what he's up to!"

Piper shrugged. Her sister had a point.

"So how do we find him?" asked Paige. "Everything you guys did before to flush him out didn't work too well."

Phoebe tapped her upper lip with her index finger as she considered the problem. "We could try scrying for him!"

"You mean like for witches?" asked Paige. "If one of us was lost or captured by the bad guys?"

"Yeah, what makes you think that would work?" asked Piper.

With a wicked grin, Phoebe said, "Well, Maxwell did lay a pretty awesome kiss on Paige before. He might have picked up some trace of her magical aura."

Paige grinned. "I *do* leave an impression. . . ."

"Fine, sure, worth a shot, I guess," Piper said. "But what do we use for a map?"

In moments, the witches stood over the long table that mirrored the house's dimensions.

"The mansion's one big rectangle, just like this table," Phoebe said, whipping a tablecloth over it and jotting the word "basement" on it.

With her sister's help, she placed three more tablecloths down, each marked to represent one of the mansion's three stories. Phoebe withdrew her scrying crystal and dangled it over the table's center. For several long moments, nothing happened, and Piper became fidgety.

"Wait for it . . . ," Phoebe coaxed. She squeezed her eyes shut and let the house's power flow through her. Then, with a lightning-like jolt, the crystal jerked down and to one side as three layers of tablecloths whipped free of the table, plucked away as if by invisible hands, and the crystal nearly dug a groove in the table as it struck home.

"That must have been *some* kiss," Piper said, impressed. She scrutinized the cloth. "Y'know, a 'You Are Here' would have been nice."

Phoebe tapped a spot just to the side of the crystal. "We're over here, practically right on top of where the ghost's hiding."

"You think he's hiding?" Paige asked.

"Nasty demon barges in and takes control of the house?" Phoebe said. "If you weren't a Charmed One, what would you be doing?"

"But he's a ghost," Piper said. "What does he have to be afraid of?"

Phoebe sighed. "Scaredy-pants or no, that's where he is. So how do we get down there?"

"I could try orbing us in," Paige suggested. "I know I can't orb *away* from the house, but maybe so long as we're staying in . . ."

Piper aimed her hands at the floor. "I could just blast the floor."

"I don't think the house would appreciate that," Phoebe said. She frowned. "Isn't this room where he first appeared a bunch of times?"

"I think so," said Piper. "Why?"

"Maybe he doesn't really think of himself as a ghost," Phoebe explained. "He never actually died, after all. It could be that he's still using secret doors and stuff like that."

The sisters searched the room and soon found that one of the bookcases was set on well-oiled rollers. A hidden winding staircase led them down to a musty candlelit corridor, the tiny flames bursting to life as they approached, extinguishing themselves after they had passed.

The trail of lights led straight to a large flat wall—and stopped.

"This is it," Phoebe said, touching the wall. "He's here. Right here, on the other side of this wall!"

Piper set her hands on her hips. "Hey, actor guy."

Silence rose up and filled the hall, until finally the ghost's head popped through the wall and he said, "Sorry, ladies. No autographs. Come back another time!"

He was about to zip out of view when Piper stopped him with a firm gesture.

"Cut the hammy delivery and answer a straight question," Piper demanded.

The ghost's eyebrows shot up. "Hammy— excuse me?"

"You heard me," Piper said.

"I-I-I—" sputtered the actor.

"Yeah, we got the feeling that's all you

think about," Piper stated flatly. "Yourself."

"Who are you to speak to me this way?" demanded the spirit.

"We're witches," said Piper. "The Charmed Ones. Mean anything to you?"

The ghost hesitated. "As I said, don't expect me to give you an autograph. I don't do that anymore."

"Yeah, like 'can't,'" Paige taunted. "No hands, no body."

A chair suddenly materialized and skidded across the bare wood floor. The actor stepped from the wall and sat down. "You're wrong. You've seen that I can still affect the living world. Or have you already forgotten our big scene together? I felt your heart as we kissed."

Paige nearly blushed, which was a rarity. "He's got a point."

"Now, listen," the actor went on, neatly crossing his legs and gesturing as if he had just stepped into a meeting with a studio head, "I did your little scene and came to the rescue once tonight, and frankly, it didn't play out at all as it should have!"

"No," Piper said. "You almost hurt our friend. An Innocent."

Maxwell's spirit hung his head, his confidence draining. "I know. I didn't mean to do that."

"Of course not," Paige said. "Don't you get it? The demon was controlling you."

The ghost bolted upright in his chair. "Demon?"

"Yeah," Paige said. "Y'know, tall guy, green skin, big curving horns, cloven hooves, the whole nine yards."

"Him," the actor said, shakily. "But I thought—"

"You thought he was a creation of the house," Phoebe said insightfully, realizing what had been on the actor's mind. "And that it was cross with you. The house, that is."

He nodded. "You mean, it's not?"

Phoebe shook her head. "The house is in pain. It's in trouble. It needs our help as much as the Innocents who were taken."

Maxwell shuddered and rose to wobbly legs. "Then it's . . . what I've been seeing, feeling . . . there's really such things as—"

The ghost shrieked like a little girl and fainted dead away.

Phoebe looked down at the spirit's prone form. "Ghosts can faint?"

"This one can," Paige said, looking around for something that might help with waking the dead.

Suddenly, all three witches heard a rustling near their heels. Phoebe whirled around first and was just in time to see Maxwell dart through the wall, leaving the Charmed Ones on their own.

Chapter 9

The Charmed Ones stood outside the wall separating them from the ghostly actor's dressing room. Piper had taken the direct approach to getting back inside, and now her hands were bruised and raw from hauling at the handle and beating at the entrance. Even her throat was getting raw from all her spirited hollering as she commanded the ghost to get his ectoplasmic backside out here.

Each time Paige tried to orb inside, she found herself feeling light-headed and confused.

"The house is still partially under his control," Phoebe said. "I could feel small surges of the house's power every time you tried to orb, like it's managing to block you somehow."

"It can mess with our powers?" asked Piper.

"I don't know about that," Phoebe told her softly. "But I think it has ideas about where people can and can't go while they're inside it."

"Yes!" called the actor from deep within his

private tomb. "You three are guests here, and you should behave accordingly."

"Fine," Piper snapped. "What are you going to do to make the demon behave?"

A startled, strangled cry seeped from beneath the door. "Demon? You weren't just trying to get a rise out of me? There are *demons* in the world? Really?"

"It gets better," Phoebe proudly proclaimed. "We're witches."

"Super witches, actually," Paige chimed in. "The three most powerful on the planet. We're the Charmed Ones."

"I understand," the spirit said. "You have abilities like she who bonded me to the house. Actually, that explains quite a bit. I was wondering why you three seemed so confident that you could banish me from the house. It seems I should have been a bit more concerned. Of course, nerves might have impaired my performance. Uh—does that mean there are also headless horsemen and the undead and—"

"Yeah, you name it, it's out there," growled Piper. She tossed up her hands in frustration. "So . . . you want to get your ghostly backside out here and give us a hand or not?"

A low, throaty voice cleared itself on the other side of the musty, dusty wall. "Since you suggest I have a choice, I'll go with 'not.'"

"Whaddya mean 'not,'" demanded the outraged Piper.

A rustling came from the other side of the door. It made Phoebe picture a newspaper being unfolded. "Thank you, no, I'm good where I am, particularly with all that you told me is out there. I don't know what I'd do if some of those horrible things wanted to critique me on my performances."

Piper rubbed at her aching temples. "There's a big bad evil demony thing squatting in your house. Don't you want to do something about it?"

"You can handle it, that's fine," said the unseen spirit. "I respect the strength and authority of women, always have."

"Look, it's okay to be afraid," Phoebe coaxed.

The ghost answered flatly, "I never said I was afraid."

Piper rolled her eyes. "Ah, geez, the typical macho—"

The ghost added, "I'm terrified!"

"Oh," Paige said.

"Listen, maybe I can help," Phoebe assured the spirit. "A little trick I learned when I was going on job interviews all the time. Just pretend you're someone else. Someone you think is qualified to handle the job at hand."

The ghost snickered dryly. "You're suggesting that I act. How novel."

Piper frowned. "Okay, cut the sarcasm and get with the program here."

"Or what?" called the snarky actor's voice.

"Oh, that does it." Piper thrust out her hands suddenly—and the wall separating the Charmed Ones from the ghost exploded.

When the debris cleared, the Charmed Ones strode inside the chamber to find Maxwell pressed in the corner, hugging his knees to his chin.

"Ain't that a picture," whispered Paige.

Piper turned to Phoebe. "Are you sure we need this guy?"

"Yeah," Phoebe said quickly. "No one knows this house better than he does."

"Get off your duff, scaredy-pants," Piper said, motioning for the ghost to rise. "Your home is being attacked. We're here to do something about it. You want to help, right? I mean, it's your house."

"You three have done your best to evict me as it is," the actor sniffled. "Why should I help you?"

"Because a big bad wicked demon guy has taken control of the place," Paige explained. "Duh!"

"Nobody's bothering me," the ghost declared. "Except you three."

"Okay, so the demon hasn't gotten around to spring cleaning yet," Piper went on. "Do you really think he's going to be okay with you living under his roof? Personally, I don't think so!"

The spirit shuddered. "I don't know what you expect me to do."

"Show us around," Phoebe said. "Help us find where he's taken the Innocents."

The actor gulped. "Could I just draw you a map? I wouldn't want to get in the way. You ladies look like you have it all under control and—"

"I thought actors were fearless," Paige said, kneeling near the ghost. "I thought you welcomed any challenge, that no role was too difficult."

The ghost's dimpled chin rose. "You seek to shame me into doing what you want?"

Paige shook her head. "Nope. But I think I know what it is *you* want. You and the house both. You're looking to perform, and you want the perfect audience, one that will really appreciate your talents. This weekend, you found that. You know it's true. The only question is whether or not you're willing to fight for what you found."

Maxwell looked away. "I don't know the first thing about fighting. Except for make-believe, I've never been in a fight in my life."

"It's not so bad," Paige said. "You kinda get used to it. The important thing is remembering what you're fighting for."

The spirit nervously looked to Phoebe. "What kind of role did you have in mind for me?"

Phoebe thought about it for a moment. "Well, in all those haunted-house movies I saw when I was a kid, there would always be one guy who really knew his stuff. One guy who had all the supernatural lore down cold, who knew the history of the house, and could just go in and go straight to the heart of the disturbance and get rid of it."

"You expect me to be some kind of investigator of paranormal phenomena?" asked the spirit. "A ghost-hunting Sherlock Holmes?"

Paige nodded sharply. "That would work."

The ghost scratched his chin. "Hmmm . . . I rather like that. I shall begin with raiment."

"With Rain Man?" asked Paige.

"Clothing, attire!" Maxwell howled. "I am surrounded by plebeians."

"Now he thinks we're in Rome or something?" Paige wondered.

The ghost sighed, shaking his head, and said no more. Instead, he concentrated and suddenly he was wearing the high-collared suit of a British gentleman from the late Victorian era. A raincoat appeared and draped itself across his broad shoulders and a deerstalker cap popped over his pate and a neatly carved curling pipe was placed in his hand.

He looked every inch the part of Sherlock Holmes himself.

"And for the apparitional aspect of my new persona," he said as he rose, "voilà!"

He gestured across his chest, and the Charmed Ones realized that they could literally see right through him.

"So this means you're willing to come out of your cubbyhole?" Piper asked. "Got a whole bunch of Innocent people need saving. Kind of on the clock here."

"One thing more that shall make my new persona complete," the spirit said. "My character shall have a name, one that sounds apropos for his character, hmmm..."

Paige sighed. "He's not coming out."

"Silence!" the actor roared.

"And he's cranky," the lovely auburn-haired witch added. Paige crossed her arms over her chest and sighed. "Why are all men such babies when it comes to facing the horrible unknown that just might eat them alive? We do it, like, three or four times a week and we're fine!"

"No," the actor said in a sharp and neatly clipped English accent. "Silence is my name. I am Professor Silence, Algernon Silence, the Ghost Detective."

"Okay, Prof," Piper said. "Now can we get this show on the road?"

The quartet quickly left the actor's dressing room. He led them through a shortcut across dusty corridors, through a hidden door masked on the other side with an old grandfather clock, and up the spiraling stairs to the first floor. The ghost's semisolid hand grazed along the distinctive butternut paneling of the great oak staircase as his neatly polished shoes half passed through the plush crimson carpeting. The barest trace of a tear formed in the corner of his eye as he gazed up at the hanging chandelier that pressed down from a chain anchored three stories above.

He loves this house, Phoebe realized. *It's like a part of him.* A grim, determined look spread across the ghost's stony features, and a fiery glow suffused him as anger overtook him. Phoebe noted this too, and thought, *His aura changes depending on how he's feeling. He's like a six foot four mood ring.*

Breathing deeply—or pretending to breathe, in any case—to center himself, the actor said, "Some houses absorb the personalities, the proclivities, the tendencies, of those who live within them."

"You mean like the way dogs start to look like their masters?" asked Piper.

"Or vice versa?" quipped Phoebe.

The ghostly detective led them down the first-floor corridor, pausing to peek inside the rec room where a collection of ancient weapons still hung neatly on the wall, including samurai swords, halberds, and maces. He studied the way the waning sunlight glinted on the razor-sharpened edges of the blades and nodded. "In a way, yes. I had this house brought here from England and reassembled stone by stone. It was designed and built for one of England's greatest actors of the day. And it was passed from the hands of one actor to another with no others in between for centuries. In its heart, it holds the spirit of creation itself. It longs to perform. Like any other living being, it has a heart. A center of its power. You've seen it, you've passed it, you've stood gazing at it. You know what it must be."

Piper planted her hands on her hips and narrowed her gaze. "Look, Maxie, ya think you could just cut the act for a minute and get to it? We've got people to save, demons to vanquish. . . ."

The ghost blanched and instantly fell out of character. "My, my, yes!" he said, his fear returning, his voice squeaking and quaking with fear. "Sorry . . . Well, speaking from personal experience as a star of stage and screen, I see this guy as a ham, and I've had to deal with more than my share of those. So where would he take them for his big performance? Where else? The theater. He wants to put on a show, yes? That's what this is all about, isn't it?"

Phoebe gently drew Piper aside and whispered, "He's not going to be any help at all if he lets his fears get the better of him. Just let him stay in character. It's like his security blanket. His woobie, or whatever."

Piper saw a flood of phantom-like beads of sweat gathering at the nape of the spirit's neck and nodded.

"Professor Silence, please continue," Phoebe urged. "How can we reach the theater from here?"

The spirit abruptly straightened up, a rosy

glow spreading across his ghostly cheeks once more. His accent returned as he said, "Under ordinary circumstances it would be a simple matter of traveling down a few corridors and ascending to the second floor. But these are hardly what anyone would call ordinary circumstance. Interestingly, the house has not performed in any of the bizarre ways you described. I almost feel as if it wants to lead us to this malignancy that has taken root at its core so that we can cut away the damaged tissue and return the house to health."

"Or maybe you're our good luck charm," Paige suggested. "Can you feel anything different about the house?"

The spirit nodded gravely. "Now that I've opened myself to it, I can feel the metaphysical ectoplasmic forces gathered there in the theater. They are greater than I ever would have expected."

"Awesome," Piper said. "It's up to something real bad. Why am I not surprised. . . ."

The ghostly detective adjusted his deerstalker cap and raised his pipe, a cloud of wispy ectoplasm wafting through the air where smoke otherwise might have been. "Shall we proceed there at once? I am well prepared for whatever dangers the house may yet present."

"Actually," Phoebe said quickly, "can you get us to the kitchen and that cute little garden out back, first?"

"You wish to fortify yourself with food, drink, and the comfort of sweet fragrances before we do battle?" he asked.

"Not exactly," Phoebe said softly. "How far are we from there?"

"It's the other side of the house," he said boldy. "Follow me."

They did, and again they threaded their way through the spacious corridors and cut through the billiard room, a mirrored hall of trophies, and a chamber adorned with movie posters and acting trophies. Strangely, no lights flickered, no walls moved, slid, or breathed of their own accord, nothing reached or clawed at them from bizarre paintings, no giant insects or animals attempted to eat them.

One simple question burned in Piper's mind: *Why not?* But she didn't dare put voice to that concern because a superstitious part of her thought that such an "avenue of inquiry," as their guide would call it, was all the evil within the house was waiting for. Things were going well, and she didn't want to jinx them.

They reached the kitchen and immediately began foraging for the ingredients they needed to create a potion that would help them vanquish the evil at the mansion's heart. Piper lit the stove and set pots filled with water to boil. Paige slipped out through the side door and rooted around in the lush garden for fresh nightshade, which the Book of Shadows claimed often grew in and around most haunted houses. She soon found the bulbs that she needed, and just as she was tearing them free from their roots, she saw movement at the corner of her eye.

Paige whirled, but even in the gloom of rapidly falling night, there was little to see. A lovely old garden with a vine-covered door lay behind her, the door swung open wide, so that she could peer in at the great bushels of yellow, white, and red roses beyond.

But . . . hadn't that door been closed when she first crouched here? She couldn't remember. Rising to her feet, she peered into the house through one of the large kitchen windows and saw Phoebe suddenly spin and look her way in alarm. Paige immediately spun around, picturing all manner of demonic evil suddenly springing at her from the garden.

There was nothing to see. A slight breeze had kicked up and the door to the garden wavered slightly, but that was all.

Paige looked back to the kitchen in time to witness Phoebe's expression softening as she shrugged and turned away as if she didn't want to appear foolish.

Weird.

The chill air sliced through Paige as the wind kicked up even more, invisible hands lifting and gently caressing her hair. She shook her head, setting her do back in place, and snagged the last of the nightshade.

Paige was two steps from the door when she noticed, for the first time, that it was covered in vines.

How could I have missed that? she wondered.

Suddenly, the creeping vines . . . creeped. They moved and surged with an eerie snakelike sinuous motion. Before Paige's hand could reach the door, the creeping vines shot across the door handle and held it tight.

Paige concentrated and tried to orb herself away from danger and back into the house, but again that strange feeling of confusion washed over her. Even though she was looking right through a clear glass window into the kitchen where her sisters and the spirit puttered, she could not even orb there.

The house was preventing her from using her power.

The vines curled around her wrists and ankles, and before she could even scream, a whiplike strand of vines wrapped around her face, covering her mouth, and she was dragged struggling toward the hungry, writhing grove that had only moments ago been a lush colorful garden.

Within the kitchen, Phoebe again felt a strange prickling sensation race up along her spine, just as she had when she looked out the window a moment earlier. Only this time, that sensation was telling her to watch her back. Literally.

A mirror sat on the paneled wall just above
the sink at which she was scrubbing her hands,
and when she peered into it, she could see that
another mirror hung on the opposite wall in
nearly the identical position. She spied the
reflection of her own back in that mirror, and in
that reflection, a collection of spiders was steal-
ing up her spine.

"Yaaahhhh!" Phoebe screamed, whirling and
snatching up a spatula that she arced behind her
back and smacked and scraped herself with. She
expected to see half-maddened spiders sliding
and skittering to the floor, but not a single one
was struck from her back.

Piper bristled, "Phoebes, what on earth—"

"Get them off, get them off!" she cried.

"There's nothing there!" Piper assured her,
looking right at her back.

"But—but in the mirror, I saw . . ." Phoebe felt
around her back. Her sister was telling the truth.

Suddenly, Piper's eyes flew open wide. Her
gaze was riveted to the collection of steel pots
and pans hanging from the ceiling. Within those
perfectly polished surfaces, her own reflection
had changed horribly: Her hair was on fire, her
flesh burning away, the bone of her skull
exposed as her mouth soundlessly worked itself
up and down.

Piper whirled, instinctively raising one hand
to shelter her from the terrible illusions, and
spun to see Phoebe being lifted into the air by an

enormous old crone who looked like a witch from a nasty book of fairy tales. The witch cackled, her sores roiling over her face, and Piper gasped.

Under all the wrinkles, scars, and sores, the powerful and ugly old witch looked just like Piper.

The closest oven sprang open to reveal a roaring fire to. The old-style oven was so enormous that it could easily accommodate Phoebe's squirming, kicking form.

"It's not real!" Piper hollered.

"Sure feels real," Phoebe said, struggling to be free.

Demons born of fire leaped out of the oven—and right at Piper.

Outside, in the garden, Paige held the edge of the door in an iron grip. The vines yanked at her, and she heard a steady, hungry hiss from the garden, as if the vines truly were serpents, accompanied by the eager chomping of wet slobbering hungry maws.

A ghostly hand suddenly descended, bearing a machete. The vines wailed as they snapped back in seething, whiplike motions.

Robert Maxwell reached down, hauled Paige to her feet, and beat at the air on either side of them as the vines gave chase. The pair reached the kitchen, and Paige burst inside.

"Pot!" she hollered. A heavy pot materialized in her hand, and she wonked the enormous

witch over the head with it. Phoebe fell to the
ground as Paige spun and gestured toward
Piper, who was besieged by flying fire creatures.
"Rain of ice!"

A torrent of ice cubes appeared above the
troop of aerial flame demons and dropped upon
them. They screeched and turned to mist, vanishing.

Piper aimed her hands at the old witch, who
was coming for Phoebe once more, and willed it
to explode. The cackling hag blew apart in a
storm of ash and sparks.

Paige   looked   around.   "Hey,   where's
Maxwell? He saved me outside."

The sisters surveyed the kitchen, Piper turning off the red-hot oven. The ghost was nowhere
to be seen, which didn't mean much where
ghosts are concerned. They searched the closets,
refrigerators,   and   finally   found   the   ghost
crouched in the cupboard. Or, well, some of him
was there, anyway. The door opened onto his
sheepish face only. The rest of him must have
been phased through the storage areas beneath
the cupboard.

He cleared his throat, "Um, ah—I thought the
cause of this strange phenomena might well
have been found here. One must always elimi-
nate the obvious; then, whatever's left, however
improbable, must be true!"

"You didn't even feel it coming, did you?"
Piper asked.

The ghostly detective hung his head. "Sorry."

"I felt it," Phoebe said. "A weird twinge."

"Let's finish our potions and go," Piper said. "I don't know if the house was just taking a nap before or what, but it's certainly lively now."

Phoebe nodded sharply. She could feel the house's power gathering around them like a coming storm guided by a dark and twisted intelligence, one that would gladly reach deeply into their hearts and minds and play with them awhile before sweeping them away toward destruction. . . .

In moments the potions were completed and the ghostly detective led the Charmed Ones through a series of tight, dark, hidden corridors. Phoebe pictured the walls suddenly pressing in, squashing them like flies.

Suddenly, Piper's fingers were before Phoebe's face, savagely snapping.

"What-what-what?" asked Phoebe.

"I don't know what it is you're doing," Piper whispered fervently, "but you're giving our guide the willies!"

Phoebe looked ahead to see the ghost shuddering, quaking, and becoming so intangible that he was little more than a flickering wisp of glowing light.

"Just do your touchy-feely reassuring thing, please," Piper growled.

"Says the mother of the group," muttered Phoebe as she slipped past her sisters and went over to the spirit. "Hey, Professor, what's—"

"No, it's not working," the ghost said. It was true, his disguise had vanished, now he was simply Robert Maxwell, movie star of the past.

"What's wrong?" asked Phoebe.

"The house," he said gravely. "It's more than just my home. I'm a part of it. Or at least I have been for the last century. Now I can barely feel any connection to it at all. I've never felt so alone."

"We'll get the house back for you," Phoebe said, rubbing his ghostly shoulder. She could barely feel him, only a slight electrical tingle played over her fingertips. "I swear."

Nodding, the ghost's color flared back to a healthier glow, but he still looked shaky.

They reached the stairwell and climbed, then emerged at a landing and carefully worked their way down the hall without being attacked.

Maxwell nodded at a pair of double doors. "The theater's through there."

Piper strode boldly to the doors and whipped them open. The Charmed Ones went inside. The theater was an impressive size, yet below, the stage was empty.

Piper whirled and looked for the ghost. "Maxwell?"

"Headed for the hills, I think," said Phoebe.

A burst of energy engulfed the stage, crimson and violet lights flaring and retreating. A mist crept into view, and a familiar-looking demonic form made his entrance. The grinning demon took the stage and gestured like a Vegas magician. Suddenly, the group of terrified Innocents appeared on the stage beside him. Kevin, Cassie, and Ryan gazed at the Charmed Ones with wide, frightened eyes. Their lips moved, but no sound came from them. They battered at the walls in a mad pantomime, as if they were trapped in a great invisible prison. The other partygoers were there as well, quaking in terror and confusion.

"Welcome, Charmed Ones," he said with a great bow and flourish of his gnarly hands. Suddenly, the doors behind the witches slammed shut, their heavy bolts sliding into place and locking them up tight. "Welcome to the final performance!"

The demon had been waiting for the Charmed Ones.

It was a trap.

Chapter 10

"Wow, big scary demon guy takes the stage," Piper muttered, rewarding the monster before her with a handful of halfhearted claps. "Color me impressed."

"Did you forget why I'm here?" asked the demon. "You vanquished my brother. I want revenge!"

"Wow," Piper said, her tone mocking, her rolling eyes and snorts of laughter revealing that she was clearly unimpressed. "So you've got to hide behind a bunch of Innocents instead of facing us directly, the way your brother did. Let me guess: You would be the scrawny *little* brother, right? The baby of the family?"

The demon opened his mouth to roar in rage, but Piper silenced him with a casually upthrust hand.

"Nah, don't bother to answer," she instructed him. "I recognize a loser when I see one."

"Are you here to talk me to death?" asked

the demon. "Or will you stand up and fight?"

"Would talking you to death actually work?" asked Phoebe. "I think I broke a nail when we fought your brother. Hate to break another one!"

With a roar, the demon whipped his hands back and directed his great open palms at the Charmed Ones. A sizzling vortex of incredible power opened before him, a cyclone of supernatural energies sporting a phantasmagoria of impossible and alarming sights and sounds. Images were carried upon the swirling winds, images of batlike men carrying fiery swords; women with raking claws for fingers and writhing spitting snakes for hair; and imps, demons, and wraiths of every size and shape holding axes, spikes, and gleaming, red-hot crimson knives.

Insanely frightening places were revealed within the walls of the churning tunnel. The sisters glimpsed scenes from a thousand horror movies, many of which they had seen when peeking out from between their interlaced fingers before grainy picture tubes on old TV sets while growing up. Twisted nightmare landscapes filled with burning pits and charred black skeletal trees and eerie high houses sitting on cliffs laden with mist and overlooking a churning choppy sea, alien worlds where monstrous creatures waited. . . .

Paige reached out, ready to grab her sisters' hands and orb them away from danger before the vortex could strike and swallow them whole, but she never had the chance.

Instead, a booming, bellowing voice boldly rang out above their heads: "Who *dares* strike at those who are under my protection?"

A towering ectoplasmic form whipped into existence between the Charmed Ones and the spiraling vortex. It held the shape of a man, but it was far bigger than life. Arms and legs as wide as tree trunks flexed while eyes blazing with excitement peered out from a mask that reached down to the bridge of its nose. The giant was cloaked in silver mist with a great dark billowing cape striking high from its back.

"I am the Spirit of Adventure!" the ghostly giant hollered. "And this is *my* house!"

With an echoing laugh, the giant reached out and grasped the edges of the oncoming cyclone, his fingers closing on the funnel with incredible strength, and he forced his end shut.

Ahead, the demon shrieked in surprise and rage as all the illusions it had been prepared to loose on the Charmed Ones instead rocketed back and struck it with full force. Suddenly, a multitude of nightmarish creatures set upon the demon, tearing and shredding at the evil mastermind, threatening to tear him right out of existence.

"Well, what do you know?" asked the titanic spirit as it shrunk down to the size of a mortal man and once again took on the visage of Robert

Maxwell. "There really is no difference between playing a hero and being one. You simply have to believe in the role!"

The whirling vortex engulfing the demon abruptly vanished. It looked up and spat dark, inky blood at Maxwell, who flinched, his pale form suddenly turning a dozen shades paler.

"Count yourself lucky that I am more interested in the witches than you," the demon said. "Your demise will be quick."

The demon gestured, and a wall of flame suddenly sprang up and overwhelmed the actor. Paige leaped forward, reaching out to snatch Maxwell and orb him away, but he screamed and burst into crimson, violet, and amber ash before she could reach him. Only a cloud of slowly falling cinders was left to mark his passing.

"Actors," the demon spat.

"You killed him," Piper said, astonished. "You killed a ghost!"

"I banished him from the house," the demon spat. "He has moved on to his final reward, whatever that might be. Oblivion, most likely, as he never truly died, and his spirit was bound to this place for eternity."

"You really are a major-league creep," Phoebe said. "Robert Maxwell was worth a thousand of you. And he had the guts to prove it too."

"Guts, yes," the demon chittered. "They burned up first."

Paige shuddered. "Is it just me, or was that

about an eleven on the one-to-ten scale for *ewww*?"

"There's nothing we can do for Maxwell now," Piper put in. "There are still Innocents here, and we have to save them."

"Yeah, and kick that thing's wrinkly backside," Paige added.

Phoebe nodded sharply. "Kick, bend, twist, fold—pick your poison."

The demon welcomed them with open arms. "Come, witches. Try your worst."

The Charmed Ones attacked as one. Phoebe levitated high, pounding the demon back with a series of high kicks to the face, while Paige summoned a mace from the rec room and smashed at the beast's ribs and knees. As the demon fell, Piper jammed her hands into the air and her sisters fell back, clearing the area.

The demon didn't explode.

"Bad demon, bad!" Piper said, snatching a potion from her pocket and gesturing for her sisters to draw near. "You should have just exploded when I told you to. Now you're really in for it. Ladies, it's Power of Three time!"

As the demon dragged itself to its unsteady haunches, the Charmed Ones began to chant:

We sisters three will vanquish thee,
Your illusions will not avail,
By the Power of Three we swear to see,
You pass beyond the veil.

Piper threw the potion.

Paige drew a sharp breath as she stared into the demon's eyes and realized that something was terribly wrong. It wasn't startled or worried in the least. In fact, it seemed to welcome the destroying potion.

Guided by instinct, Paige drove her hand out and yelled, "Potion, away from him!"

An instant before the potion would have struck the demon's heavily muscled hide, the small glass vial veered off, as if snatched by an invisible hand, and whisked its way against a heavy wood support beam just offstage and exploded harmlessly.

The demon shrugged. "Pity."

The "demon" transformed, its fearsome features melting like wax, its skin becoming flesh-colored, hair sprouting up over its bald, scarred pate as its horns retreated. Its dark eyes filled with a familiar blue, and its body was suddenly clothed in a well-worn pair of blue jeans while its cloven hooves morphed into human feet with cute, well-manicured toes, two of which bore rings Paige remembered.

"Craig!" she hollered.

Craig stared at Paige blankly before collapsing. Paige ran to Craig and knelt beside him. His chest rose and fell, his breathing shallow, but steady. Cradling his head in her lap, she caressed his cheeks and tried to wake him, but he was out cold. The spell had not harmed him, but he was drained from his ordeal. She ran her hand over his bare ribs, which Paige had pummeled with the mace, but those blows had not injured him. The demon must have given him strength and protection so that the ruse would appear convincing.

Paige eased Craig's sleeping form back onto the stage and she stepped away from the fallen hottie.

The unseen demon's voice came from everywhere and nowhere at once. "Did you forget that I am a master of illusions? I made Craig look just like me in the hope that you witches would vanquish an Innocent. That mistake would have destroyed your proud spirits and preyed upon your consciences for the rest of your days . . . not that I planned for you to live long, anyway. I just wanted to see your anguish. Ah, well, there are other ways to make you witches suffer."

The demon snapped his fingers, and the gathered Innocents shattered like images in crazy funhouse mirrors—which is exactly what they were, just another illusion.

"I've hidden the rest of the partygoers elsewhere," said the demon. "But you see now that I can take their lives whenever I wish, and I will do just that if you witches refuse me in any way."

The demon gestured, and a maze of mirrors appeared around the sisters. These were not funhouse mirrors, though. The reflections were not distorted or exaggerated in any way. Their ornate gold and silver casings gleamed in the soft golden glow from the stage lights, and within each polished surface stood perfect mirror images of the Charmed Ones.

"Wow," Piper said, planting her hands on her hips. "You're going to destroy us by making us stare into mirrors and wish we'd put on more makeup, or not worn this outfit today? Sheesh, I—"

Piper abruptly spun back to the nearest mirror as she realized that her reflected image had not mimicked her movements at all. It had stood stock-still, not placing its hands on its hips when she had, not moving when she had.

And her mirror image bore a wicked and evil grin.

"Hoo-boy," Piper whispered.

Paige and Phoebe had also noticed the strange way their reflections had not moved with them.

Suddenly, one of the reflected Phoebes looked back at the real Phoebe and said, "Girl, you've been putting on weight."

"No, I haven't!" Phoebe roared. Then she looked down at her bare midriff and rock-hard abs, anyway.

"Made ya look!" taunted Phoebe's mirror image.

And a mirror-Paige added, "Tell it to me

straight, Paigey-poo. Is there even *one* of these guys you met this weekend you haven't had naughty thoughts about? Your sisters were so right about you, and they were being kind. You're not just man-crazy, you're a man-eater."

"Am not!" Paige said. "I've been good all weekend."

"Maybe," said the mirror-Paige. "But only because you've been working hard at it. You'll be yourself again any minute . . . or maybe you won't. Not if we have anything to say about it."

A legion of illusionary Charmed Ones stepped out from the mirrors and stalked toward the three witches. The mirrors vanished behind them.

"I don't have to destroy you," the demon bragged. "You will destroy one another!"

Phoebe smirked. She wasn't going to let any of this worry her. These other versions of the Charmed Ones were just mirror images—illusions. "They can't hurt us!" Phoebe boasted.

A boot that was every bit as solid as the one Phoebe was wearing suddenly soared high and smacked Phoebe in the side of her head, rocking her from her feet. One of the duplicates had *kicked* her!

Two more doubles leaped high into the air, delivering spinning kicks that caught Phoebe's jaw and chest. With a groan, Phoebe collapsed, her head throbbing, stars exploding before her eyes as painful bruises already began to take hold.

"They've got our powers," Paige said as she reached for Phoebe. With a grunt of effort, Paige helped the frowning Phoebe to her feet.

"Owww," Phoebe muttered, moving her jaw from side to side. "I think that loosened some of my fillings."

Piper raised an eyebrow. "He can make illusions turn solid, just like his brother. That means any of these duplicates can hurt us—or worse."

Paige looked at her sisters with determination. "We'll be fine, so long as the three of us true Halliwells stick together."

The demon laughed again. "As if I would make it that easy for you . . ."

Suddenly, the great stage whirled. Piper and her sisters felt their heads spinning as the world became a startling blur. Piper instinctively reached out for her sisters, but her hands came up empty. Squinting open a single eye, Piper saw her sisters reaching out for her, as well, their eyes open and imploring.

In fact, she saw a few too many of her sisters.

She blinked—and there were four Phoebes before her.

Again she blinked—and two dozen Paiges surrounded her.

A third blink—and she found herself staring into her own incredulous face.

She squeezed her eyes shut as the world kept spinning. Then, at last, it slowed and stopped. Piper opened her eyes and found herself in the theater's long, tilting center aisle, her sisters standing directly before her.

Only . . . were they really her sisters?

Evil laughter erupted from the duo as they eased toward her.

"Wait, stop!" Piper hollered, but it was no use. Her sisters were on the attack—and she was the enemy.

Chapter 11

Piper leaped back and to one side as Phoebe's boot whooshed through the air, missing her by inches, the fierce roar and rush of wind exploding in her ear. Her sister's high kick had been aimed at Piper's face, and she had barely avoided the blow.

"Lamp!" Paige called, and a large brass lamp from the study appeared in her hand. Before Piper could regain her wits, Paige swung the lamp at her stomach, driving the wind from her and doubling her over.

Phoebe's knee savagely snapped up, catching the underside of Piper's jaw and whipping her back, arms flailing, to land flat on her back.

The sisters gathered over the fallen Piper.

"Thought she'd put up more of a fight," Phoebe said.

"She probably figured we wouldn't dare punch her lights out," Paige said with a snicker. "You know she always expects us to just do whatever she says."

"Bossy little witch," Phoebe said.

Shaking her head, Piper rose to one knee and smiled. "Thanks, ladies. That's what I needed to hear to know you two definitely aren't my sisters."

Her hands thrust out, her fingers flying wide, and the pair of evil duplicates exploded.

Just as suddenly as they had disappeared, three more sets of Paiges and Phoebes appeared in their place. But each of these looked surprised and disoriented. Each set of sisters quickly regained their bearing and drew back from one another in surprise and alarm.

"Phoebe, get behind me," one of the Paiges said, worriedly eyeing the other sets of witches and Piper.

"Paige, get behind *me*," one of the Phoebes responded.

Not gonna make it that easy anymore, is he? Piper thought. These duplicates, if they were duplicates, were acting a lot more like her true sisters.

More and more sets of bewitched and bewildered Phoebes and Paiges settled around Piper, who drew in a breath and looked at each one, trying to find some clue regarding which just might be the real thing—and which might attack at any moment.

Then the ring of sisters drew closer, closer still, the duplicates' voices rising to a pressing, swelling tide, and Piper heard one of them—

who knows which it might have been—holler, "Sword!"

A flash of steel glinted, and from between the crush of witches, Piper spied a speeding sword flying at her chest.

A dozen yards away in the darkened theater, Phoebe faced Paige. Or was it Paige?

"How do I know you're my sister?" Phoebe asked.

"What—you want to know what you were thinking about getting up to that one summer when the family went to that farm in Iowa for an outing and you met the neighbor's son out behind the woodpile?" asked Paige.

"I, uh—huh, what?" Phoebe cried. "Paige wouldn't know anything about that. We didn't grow up together."

"You talk in your sleep," Paige said, rolling her eyes. "And you kept nodding off on the drive over here."

Phoebe relaxed. "Okay, so let's find Piper and—"

"Anvil," Paige said with a whisper of casual malevolence.

A high, sharp whistling from above alerted Phoebe just in time. She dove out of the way as the anvil smashed the floor where she had stood a split-second earlier.

"Paige" haughtily strode closer. She laughed and called, "Frogs!"

A rain of frogs flopped down onto Phoebe,

keeping her off-balance and icked out as the fake Paige slinked ever nearer.

"How did you know about Iowa?" Phoebe demanded.

"You talk in your sleep," Paige said. "And you've slept here, in the house. How do you think? Hmmm, oil slick."

A sudden black pool of slippery liquid appeared beneath Phoebe's feet just as she swept up with one boot and attempted to kick the fake Paige into next Thursday. She slipped on the oil spill, her feet flying up, the back of her skull and her shoulder blades hitting the floor first as she fell.

"Owwww," Phoebe groaned.

"Beretta 9.2 self-loading repeating submachine gun," Paige said, stifling a yawn.

Phoebe stiffened—but nothing appeared in Paige's hands.

The fake Paige smirked. "Just kidding. I'm limited to things that are actually in the house. Like—ceiling!"

Phoebe rolled and tried to get out of the way in time, but she could get no traction whatsoever as a torrent of debris rained down on her from above.

Near the "gods"—the uppermost rows of seats in the theater—the real Paige looked down in horror as her sisters were besieged by badness. She had suddenly found herself among a crushing horde of other Paiges and a ton of

Phoebes, with Piper only an arm's length away. She had reached for Piper even as she heard another Paige call for a sword, and saw the weapon flash at her sister. But someone knocked her out of the way just as she summoned an orb and tried to grab her sister, and so she had teleported to safety alone.

Or had she?

Paige looked down and saw Piper lying a few feet away. "Piper!"

Descending on her sister, Paige checked Piper for sword wounds and found none. She gathered Piper into her arms and hugged her close.

"I was so worried!" Paige cried.

"Huh," Piper said, coming around. "Then you really are a sucker."

The phony Piper's knee came up into Paige's ribs, driving her back, and the double whipped her hands around, summoning her power to blow things up and aiming it right at Paige.

The demon laughed as he watched the witches battle. Suddenly, he felt an odd tingle of energy from the cages in which he had secured the humans. Turning from the witches for an instant, he looked in on his prisoners.

The mortals were being kept not just in physical restraints, but also in secure prisons of illusion. Each believed that he or she was somewhere quite far from here, leading a happy life.

In his world of illusion, Ryan sat back on a

throne in a great palace, hundreds of women bringing him food and wine and attending his every need. He had seized absolute control of his family's fortune and had exiled all his relatives to an estate on an island in the Caribbean. Free to do exactly what he wanted whenever he wanted, he led a life of debauchery and excess rarely known in the modern age.

In Karl's fantasy world he had become the next billionaire "geek" entrepreneur and was running countless business empires.

Craig, in his fantasy, was the world's most beloved comedic film actor, making people laugh and feel good about themselves wherever he went.

And young Cassie, well . . . the demon sighed. He had seen enough. All of the prisoners looked secure. The chains binding their sleeping forms were locked tight, and each was lost in their own private worlds.

Had he looked a moment longer, however, he might have seen the first glimmers of what might prove to be his ultimate undoing.

In her life of illusion—though it seemed entirely real to her—Cassie leaned back in her box seat at the Peking Opera, anxiously awaiting the arrival of her loving husband. She surveyed the crowd below as they hurried to their seats, the vast orchestra tuning up for the night's performance, the conductor taking his place. Her Vera Wang original had earned her a number of compliments, and she'd graciously allowed more than a dozen photographers to collect her image. She knew that her presence here tonight meant a good deal to Ryan's latest round of deal-making, and she intended to help him any way she could. And later, they would laugh at all the silly, formal, showy things they had to do to cinch these billion-dollar deals that would help so many poor and underprivileged families.

It was a good life . . . no, a fabulous one. The jet-setting was fun, the glitz and glamour a dazzling enough thing onto itself, but what truly mattered was that she and Ryan were one heck of a team. She had married a man who not only held the power to make a difference in the world, but had the vision and inner strength to wield it wisely. In ten short years Ryan had transformed his family's holdings into the third biggest commercial venture in the world, and he had single-handedly sponsored research that was already solving issues of world hunger, disease, and energy.

She was never just the "little woman" either. They both led and inspired by example, as she served as both an activist, social reformer, and mother of two. Best of all, she hadn't been forced to give up one shred of who she was and what she believed in. Her hair was still streaked and crazy, her piercings pronounced.

"You can't change the world," Ryan had told the press countless times. "But you can make the world curious, and it just may change of its own accord to be more like you, or to embrace the options you present."

She wondered exactly how long it would be before he ran for the presidency, as so many of his people had been suggesting for the last several years. . . .

"Pardon me, ma'am," said a woman wearing a kimono, a black silken wig, and thick, pale traditional powdered makeup. A small silver tray was in her hands, and resting upon that tray, a note. "A message for the respected one."

"Thank you," Cassie said, picking up the folded sheet of high-quality linen paper. By the time she unfolded it, the messenger was gone. Cassie's brow furrowed as she read the words on the note.

noisulli na si efil ruoy

Cassie had learned dozens of languages, but she didn't know this one. Or did she? A memory from childhood suddenly came to her. She was passing notes in class in code.

This was English, the message was simply written exactly backward. She would need a mirror to read it easily.

Digging her compact from her purse, Cassie held the note up to it and read:

your life is an illusion

And in the depths of the mirror, Cassie saw images forming. Images from that night so long ago, when she realized that the only man who might have stolen her from Ryan's arms was rotten to the core. But these images were of Ryan and Karl setting the trap that had ensnared Kevin. They were the ones who took delivery of the machines that generated the smoke and heated the door without setting it ablaze. They had greased the vines and locked Craig and Jessica into that room.

Her husband had nearly murdered her! Kevin was innocent.

"No," she whispered. "It's a trick."

"This is the trick," whispered the woman who had delivered the message. She was behind Cassie now, holding the mirror in place. "Everything you're experiencing right now is a lie, an illusion, and it's of your own making. As evil and selfish as Ryan was when he set up that poor boy who loves you, the thing that's making all this seem real for you is a thousand times worse. It's using you. It's using the power of the illusions you're keeping about this man to trap you here so you'll never ever escape, never even want to. Don't let that happen. Don't let it win. You can beat this thing."

Cassie shuddered. "How?"

The woman gestured, and far below, the audience was gone, it was literally washed away by a great, deep pool of sparkling moonlit water.

"Face your illusions," the woman said. "Dive deep into the thing you're terrified to know, and then what's trapped you here won't have any power over you."

Cassie's fingers let go of the mirror, and the messenger let it drop as well. The small compact tumbled end over end, splashing down into the pool far below. Cassie gasped, her fear gripping her as she looked away from the water.

"You won't be hurt," the woman promised. "You won't drown. See? The man who should have saved you is there, waiting."

Forcing herself to gaze into the impossible water, Cassie saw Kevin deep within them, smiling up at her.

"He's what's real," the messenger said. "Not any of this."

Somehow, deep down, Cassie felt that what the woman said was true. She looked down at her hand and saw that it no longer bore a wedding ring. And her two children . . . she didn't know their names, or if she'd given birth to boys or girls.

She had been tricked.

"I'll do it," Cassie said, rising to the balcony box and bravely readying herself to jump.

Her eyes open wide, Cassie felt the chains binding her in the physical world fall away as she leaped into Kevin's waiting arms. She woke within the physical prison in which the demon had kept her and the others, and quickly went to work waking and freeing the others.

• • •

Meanwhile, amidst the ever-shrinking ring of fake Phoebes and Paiges, the true Piper once again narrowly slid out of the way of the gleaming sword, which drove from one direction, then the other, as the fake Paiges started orbing in and out of existence with breathtaking speed.

Piper's hand itched to start blowing up the doubles, but there were so many of them, none of which she would see making a hostile move toward her, and it was possible that her real sister was truly in the midst of all this madness.

All of a sudden, yet another Paige orbed in next to Piper, threw her arms around her, and orbed them both out just as the blade struck where Piper's heart had been. The shining blue-white energies of the orb faded, and Piper saw that she and Paige were crouched in the wings backstage. From here, they could see all the madness below.

"All that rubble, that must be where they cornered Phoebe," Paige said, rising and taking a bold step away.

Piper's hand shot up and gripped her wrists. "Waitaminute. How do I know you're the real Paige?"

Paige shrugged. "You don't. I guess you'll just have to trust me."

"Good enough," Piper said quickly. She had the feeling that the demon's duplicates wouldn't know the first thing about love and trust, so she was willing to take the chance that this really was her sister.

Paige orbed to the spot where other fake Paiges were unearthing the rubble. Phoebe's still form was half exposed.

"Pathetic," the closest of the fakes said to her, mistaking her for another of their unearthly brethren of illusions made real. "I thought she would have put up more of a fight."

"You mean like this?" Paige asked. "Two-by-four!"

The heavy wooden plank appeared in her hands. She swept it in a wide, punishing arc, knocking out two copies of herself with one swing. The other was about to open her mouth to summon something when Paige drove the two-by-four into her stomach. Another "Paige" rushed at her from behind, but a high, sharp *crack* sounded, and she collapsed at the real Paige's feet.

Paige spun to see Phoebe standing before her.

"Witches, magic?" Phoebe muttered. "Like all I'm good for is high kicks? I don't think so. I've been keeping a charged shield bracelet and other goods in my pocket for a while now, just in case. That's what kept the debris from crunching me."

"I'm the real Paige," Paige whispered.

"Then orb us out of here," Phoebe suggested.

Paige took her hand and orbed them to the wings, where Piper waited. Then she spun and drew in a deep breath, as if she was about to orb away again, but this time on her own.

"Wait, where are you going?" Phoebe asked urgently.

Paige's gaze narrowed. "To finish this."

"Sure you don't need help?" asked Piper.

"Better this way," Paige assured her. She summoned the orb and vanished in a shower of blue-white sparks.

Paige reappeared beside the fake Piper she had left in the theater's uppermost rows of seats.

"Come on," she said, grabbing "Piper's" arm. "They're getting away!"

She orbed again, this time taking them right into the middle of the doppelgänger pack.

"That one," Paige said, pointing at a pack of fake Phoebes. "That's the real Phoebe."

"Which one?" asked the phony Piper.

Paige shrugged, her heart thundering. "Not sure now, but she's in there, so get 'em all!"

Piper raised both of her hands, and the fake Phoebes began exploding en masse. Just as Paige had expected, the duplicates had no trouble destroying one another if it meant a chance at the real thing.

"Hmmm, may have spoken too soon, try that batch over there," Paige said, pointing at more fake Phoebes and Paiges.

The phony Piper raised her hands again, blowing up the new group.

"Better get 'em all, just to be sure," Paige said.

"Piper" unleashed her power at the swarming, snarling mass of fakes, blowing them all to bits.

"That did it," Paige said. "Now let's take you back to the master." Paige grabbed the phony's arm and orbed her back to the spot where she first encountered the duplicate.

"Hey, waitaminute," the fake Piper said, slowly catching on that she had been duped—and had been used to destroy the other copies.

Paige didn't give the duplicate a minute. Instead, she tried a final desperate maneuver, gripping the fake Piper's arm, driving her toward the wall, and partially orbing them *into* it. Paige let go just as the wall solidified around them, but the howling fake Piper was trapped. She exploded as she became a solid form within the wall.

"Huh," Paige said, clasping her hands. "And who said I never paid attention in science class. No two objects can occupy the same space at one time, not without something blowing up. There ya go."

She orbed back to the wings and picked up her sisters.

"All clear," Paige declared.

"How about getting us out of here, then?" asked Phoebe. "We need to get reinforcements, and more ingredients for potions."

Paige took both of their hands and orbed once more, but she only made it so far as the first row of seats before the theater stage. A spotlight flared to light, and a brilliant circle of illumination was seared onto the stage. Applause rose from a single pair of clapping hands, and the theater was filled with a dark, rolling laughter that could only belong to one unimaginably evil creature.

A form materialized, one the Charmed Ones recognized at once.

The demon had come for them, this time in the flesh. Phoebe in particular could sense his daunting physical presence somehow reaching out and filling the theater as if by force of will alone.

Kevin, Cassie, and Ryan lay upon the stage around him.

Cassie stirred and shrank back from Ryan as if he were the most loathsome thing she had ever seen in her life. Kevin reached for her instinctively, and she pressed herself to him.

"Impossible!" roared the demon. "They have awakened from their illusions. Which of you did this? How could you have entered the illusion I cast for her from her own desires? I will destroy you for this!"

"Do you have the first idea what he's talking about?" asked Piper.

"Not so much," responded Paige.

"He's vulnerable," Phoebe said. "Something happened, and it weakened him."

"I'll get her back!" the demon screamed. "She

must be under my control. Her illusions were so sweet, so powerful . . . I will have her, I swear."

"Yeah, well, in the meantime, why don't you try us on for size, pal," Piper said defiantly.

"Brave words," the demon replied. "But that's all they are. Words. You will need more than that to defeat me."

"Oh, we've got more, don't you worry about that," Paige said bravely. Her expression faltered as she looked to her sisters. "We do, right?"

"You're the one who said it," Phoebe muttered under her breath.

"Of course we do," Piper said. "Paige, orb out of here and come back with help!"

Paige nodded sharply, and a shimmering field of blue-white light crackled into view around her. She vanished—and reappeared instantly. "No can do," Paige said. "Something's preventing me from leaving the theater."

"That would be me," the demon said. "You must stay for the final performance!"

"This isn't just about revenge for your brother, is it?" asked Phoebe. "You've got the power of the house to draw on, you could have used it to capture us one by one before we even knew you were here. What is it you're really after?"

"Domination, of course," said the laughing demon. "First, of the human world, naturally enough. I will become one with Ryan. His illusions about his own unstoppable power call to me, as do his position of wealth and power in your human world. The girl will live. She is necessary to become his paramour and maintain his position with his family . . . a family that will soon, one member at a time, meet with many unfortunate accidents until only Ryan is left to control their empire. The writer, Kevin . . . his illusions about the woman, that she could ever truly love him, gave me a hold on his soul, and on this house. He will have his uses, as well."

"Come on, that's it?" asked Piper. "You want to be a big hotshot media mogul?"

"Through this 'media' you speak of, I will filter illusions of my own making into the consciousness of all humanity," the demon went on. "Enslaving humanity in that manner is but my first step. Before long, I will rule the Underworld with even more power at my command than the Source. This house will be my 'recruiting station' for my legions of human warriors. I will use it to trap humans into worlds made of their own precious illusions, then I will command them to take little bits of this house into the world to enslave others to my will, a process that will be helped by my 'media empire.' Soon, all of humanity will be my legion of warriors, billions of flesh-and-blood slaves that I will use to force open the gates of the Underworld and help me seize what is rightfully mine—and that of my besmirched family."

"You didn't just use 'besmirch' in a sentence,

did you?" asked Piper. "I mean, that's, like, out of bounds and over the top even for mondo-super baddies."

The demon threw his head back and laughed again. "You seek to rile me, but I will not fall for your pitiful schemes. Instead, I will—"

"You will do nothing, you miserable, hated wretch," said a booming, malevolent voice. "Except turn and face your destiny—and your doom!"

The Charmed Ones could not see who—or what—had made the bold and terrifying promise. Yet Phoebe was close enough to see that a look of total terror had stolen upon the demon's face as it beheld the bearer of that voice.

Chapter 12

The illusions fell, and the vast theater returned. Phoebe's eyes widened in shock as she saw the demon on his knees, clutching his skull, high piteous wails tumbling from his lips. His gaze was fixed on the floor. He could not lift his head to gaze fully at the creature who towered above him. But Phoebe recognized the newcomer at once.

"Whoa!" Phoebe said. "That's the demon we vanquished in Chinatown just before we came here. It's that guy's brother!"

"Can't be," Piper whispered. "Not unless it's a—"

"A ghost," Paige finished. "This house does have its share of them."

"Fool!" swore the ghostly newcomer. "You were supposed to avenge my destruction. Even in death I am forced to appear and fix your ridiculous mistakes."

"No, my brother, no!" the demon howled. "You do not understand."

"Of course I do," spat the demon spirit. "You placed your own ambition, your own dreams of power and glory, over fulfilling your obligation to your blood. You are unworthy of your name, and the name of our clan."

"No!" the demon wailed. "I will destroy the Charmed Ones. I—I only wanted to make them suffer first, for the torment they fostered upon you."

"Do you understand nothing?" the ghostly demon snarled. "By toying with the witches, you give them time to gather their power and devise a plan to defeat you."

"Point," Phoebe said.

The still-living demon fell to his knees, his hands outstretched imploringly. "My brother, please, I beg you—forgive me."

"I cannot," said his brother. "You have failed in life as I failed in death. A curse be on our houses!"

The living demon buried his face in his hands and wailed in torment, his cries a deafening roar of agony.

The ghostly "demon" glanced over to the Charmed Ones—and winked. His "demonic" visage wavered for a moment, revealing his true face.

It was Maxwell!

He wasn't destroyed after all! Paige realized. She gasped as a delicate finger tapped her on the shoulder from behind.

Whirling, Paige confronted the unexpected sight of Emily, the ageless witch who had cast a spell on Maxwell in the first place. Emily placed a finger over her mouth for silence. There would be time for explanations later.

She must have been the one who broke Cassie free from the demon's illusions, Paige realized. *And that helped weaken him enough to give us a fighting chance against him.*

Emily stood back and sang another spell, this one in barely a whisper. *"To the Sisters Three, I give to Thee, a boon I once granted, to you-know-He!"*

"'You-know-He'?" asked Piper. "That's not grammatical."

"No," Phoebe added. "But I think it's going to work!"

The Charmed Ones felt incredible power surge through them. Suddenly, each one of them felt as if she were one with the house. Phoebe's sensitivity to the great power of the house was intensified a thousandfold and shared by her sisters. They suddenly felt the tiny tapping of a spider's leg at the corner of the attic ceiling, a slight draft in the downstairs kitchen, a creak from the floorboards of the bowling lanes as the house shuddered and tensed for battle.

Even more palpably, they could feel the magnificent surge of power the house possessed, the vast magical well the demon had tapped into for his own dark ends. The power rushed through them, pouring over them in waves, drowning and devouring them at first, then gently rushing through them as quickly and surely as the pounding blood in their veins.

Emily had given them the same access to the powers of the house that she had granted Maxwell, only she hadn't had to make the sisters cross over to the next life to do it.

"Hey, I've been practicing," Emily said with a wink. Then she leaned back and placed her hand on what she thought was a seat-back to balance herself while she tried to strike a casual pose—and yelped as her hand gripped empty air a few inches from the chair and she flopped back onto her butt.

And the Smooth Move Award goes to . . . , Paige thought, then she chided herself. *Emily may have two left feet, but she did give us access to all this power.*

"Innocents!" Paige shouted, thrusting her hand before her. A blinding blue-white orb blossomed before her, and a small group of partygoers materialized.

Whoa, I can't remember the last time I had power like this behind me, Paige thought. "Outside, to safety! Go!"

Before the demon could object, Paige had orbed the partygoers out of the house and beyond his reach to safety.

Only Kevin, Cassie, and Ryan remained. The demon's hold on them had been too strong for Paige.

"You can use the house's power as well," the demon said warily, looking beyond his "brother" at the Charmed Ones and their clumsy witch companion. "But I have been here longer, I have been studying it, attenuating my abilities with it, and—"

"Brother!" bellowed the apparition of the demon's brother. "Why have you ceased prostrating yourself before me? Wail and beat your breast, foul fiend, pitiful excuse for a—"

The demon gestured—and Robert Maxwell's demonic disguise fell away. The demon roared at the affront. "You would dare desecrate the memory of my brother, who is your superior in every way, you pitiful piece of ectoplasmic filth?"

"There was *nothing* pitiful about that performance," the ghostly actor proclaimed. "I had you in tears, and we both know it. I'd say it was my crowning achievement."

"Very well," the demon said, his hands suddenly wreathed with arcane amber energies. "Then here is your compensation, *actor*."

The demon's hand whipped back and shot forward, the amber energies hurtling at the ghost.

Piper's hands flew up before her, and with all her might, she called on the power of the house to boost her own abilities and willed the torrent of magical energies to freeze. The flood of crackling energy suddenly solidified, but its momentum would not be stopped. It sped forward like a glowing amber spear, and drove itself at Robert Maxwell's heart.

Fortunately, he vanished a moment before it could strike.

"Thanks for slowing that down," his echoing voice called from everywhere and nowhere within the theater at once. "If you ladies don't mind, I think it really is time for me to dash. Need to prepare for my next scene and—"

"Great job, Maxwell," Paige called. "We've got it from here."

The soft, billowing wind that had carried the actor's words fell away, and he was gone.

"Actually, I think you guys could have used him," Emily said, blowing the bangs from before her face as she joined the Charmed Ones. "But I guess with him gone, the job of keeping our pal busy while *you three* do what you need to do falls to me."

Paige caught the strong inflection on those two little words. *You three?* What was Emily trying to tell them?

Ryan's limp form suddenly rose high above the stage, as if drawn up on the invisible wires of a puppeteer. The demon gestured, and Ryan's form sailed toward him.

"We will be one," the demon vowed. "And then the witches will not dare to move against me. You may be a wretch in your way, human, but you are still an Innocent, and that Innocent part of you will be kept alive within me to ensure they cannot vanquish—"

"You know, you bad guys are pretty lame sometimes," Emily said, suddenly levitating between the demon and his intended victim. A bolt of white light burst from her, creating a magical cage around Ryan, holding him just out of the howling demon's reach. "It's all, blah-blah-blah, let me tell you my evil plan, here's how I'm gonna make mincemeat out of mankind, and all that whatnot. If you just shut up and did something for once, instead of being so in love with the sound of your voice, you probably wouldn't get your heads handed to you, like, I dunno—every time."

The demon said nothing. He merely glared at the witch, then shot forward and snatched her up by the hair. She screeched, grabbing his thorny wrists as he shook her wildly.

"Whoa, hey, cut it out, hair pulling, not in the rulebook!" she yowled.

"There are no rules when it comes to this!" the demon howled. His hand suddenly became immaterial, and he thrust it into her chest. Emily bucked and shrieked, then fell quiet and unmoving as the demon drew out a shining white matrix of power. "I will consume . . . no, wait. I'll just do it."

Before the Charmed Ones could mount an attack, the demon *ate* the glowing matrix of power and dumped the still-breathing but otherwise still form of the century-old witch to the floor. He laughed as the power he had taken from her surged through him.

"There!" the demon snarled.

"Do you notice anything funny?" asked Paige as she brushed up against Phoebe.

"Like how icky it is to watch a demon eat a witch's power?" Phoebe asked.

"No," Piper cut in, "like how that magical cage around Ryan is still in place, even with Emily supposedly powerless. It's almost like . . ."

The demon took a powerful stride forward— and fell off the stage, dropping flat onto his face.

He howled in pain and rage as he reached for a chair back and tried to rise. But he missed the chair with his thorny hand and stumbled, smacking his head on an armrest. A scream of frustration rose from the demon.

"Emily said she'd keep him busy," Phoebe said. "She gave him some of her power all right, and *all* of her clumsiness. But how are we going to—"

Paige suddenly understood what Emily had been trying to tell them. "We need to try another Power of Three spell!"

"The last one didn't work," Piper pointed out.

Paige nodded. "I know, but we didn't have the power of the house behind us then."

Also on the stage, Kevin and Cassie stirred. The demon whirled at them, laughing. "Your pitiful illusions about your lives have given me great power, and the way into the very soul of he who will be my mortal host. Now it is time to strip you both of your last illusions—that you are anything more than pawns to my power."

Kevin seemed to sense what was happening, a part of him simply knew that the demon was going to place him in danger to keep the Charmed Ones occupied while he found a way to break Ryan free from Emily's cage.

"Cassie, I love you," he said quickly. "Always have, always will. Maybe I was kidding myself, believing that deep down you felt the same way about me, but I'm telling you right now, what I feel isn't an illusion."

She nodded gravely, still stinging over Ryan's many betrayals. Yet the light of hope, and even love, sparked in her dark, beautiful eyes.

The demon reached for them, but Phoebe got there first.

"You know, Emily was right," Phoebe said. "If you had just gone for it, I never could have gotten here in time. You're one yappy fella."

She levitated high and struck out with a series of punishing kicks that drove the now uncoordinated demon back. Behind her, Paige and Piper frantically worked out a final Power of Three spell.

The demon howled and waved his hands. The floor of the stage became riddled with holes that looked down onto a gaping pit filled with a churning bed of lava. The walls sprouted spikes that detached and flew at Phoebe and the Innocents, whipping, soaring, and striking just inches from their targets. A legion of giant snake-men with fangs dripping black poisonous goo appeared around the combatants.

Cassie's eyes widened in shock and horror, but Kevin drew her close, slipping his hand over her eyes.

"None of it's real," he whispered. "You're safe, none of it's real."

"Wow, you must be feeling desperate," Phoebe said. "This is all like hokey B-movie stuff!"

"And you must be forgetful," the demon added. "Will you never remember my true power?"

Some of the snake-men, whose human torsos tapered down into long, snakelike bodies while their jaws opened wide, snatched up Kevin and Cassie, while another whipped its tail at Phoebe, sweeping her legs out from under her. She fell flat on her face, the demon's hooved feet stalking near.

"I can make illusions solid and real," the demon roared. "And my power can—"

"I didn't forget anything, Chatty Cathy," Phoebe said, planting her hands on the stage and raising her head slowly to grin right into the demon's face. "The power's still coming from inside you, right? And you've still got Emily's curse of two left feet, don'tcha? So that means your creations are klutzes too."

Phoebe's arms straightened, and she whipped her legs around in a wide arc, her boots smacking toward the demon's shins. He instinctively leaped back and lost his footing, dropping with a frustrated wail into one of the potholes he had made in the floor toward the red-hot pool of lava below. He struck with a great hissing *sploosh*. But Phoebe sensed the pit wouldn't hold him for long.

"Come on, boys," Phoebe said, waving at the snake-men. "Bite me!"

They rushed at her, a dozen surging at once with wild, maniacal abandon. Even the two who had grabbed Kevin and Cassie dropped their prizes and flew at Phoebe.

With a warm smile, she drew on the power of the house and flung herself all the way to the ceiling, grabbing hold of the long steel pipe that glaring lights were mounted upon. She laughed as the snake-guys all smacked together, their skulls sounding like a rack of balls being split apart on the break at a pool hall. They sank to the ground, their writhing, sinuous bodies all sinking down into the lava pits.

One struck the demon as he tried to climb out and dragged both of them back to the fiery depths!

"Phoebes!" Piper called. "We've got it!"

Phoebe ran back to her sisters and was at

their side as the demon bounded high from the pit and dropped down before them.

"Now I shall—" he bellowed.

Piper rolled her eyes. "For once and for all, just put a sock in it."

Clasping hands, the Charmed Ones chanted:

Demon of illusion, we Sisters Three,
Call upon the house and the Power of Three!
We see right through you, and don't you know,
Where you're heading, you don't want to go.

"No, stop!" the demon cried, running toward the Charmed Ones—and tripping over his own feet. By the time he got back up to one knee, it was too late to stop the powerful witches.

Paige thrust a hand out and yelled, "Potion!"

A large, tapered glass filled with steaming liquids appeared in her hand. She and Piper had found that by simply visualizing what they desired, they could use the power of the house to create anything they wanted. While Phoebe fought the demon to keep him from the Innocents—including Ryan—invisible magical hands had been mixing the potion in the kitchen.

"No!" the demon wailed again.

Without hesitation, Paige threw the glass, which shattered at the demon's feet. A great burst of light engulfed the demon, and he exploded into a thousand shimmering, screaming shards.

On the stage, the cage around Ryan disappeared and Ryan's unconscious form flopped down even as Emily slowly stirred. Paige raised her hand and said, "Ryan! Outside!"

He vanished from the stage, and the Charmed Ones rushed to Emily's side.

"Emily, did it get all your power?" asked Paige.

The kooky witch raised an eyebrow. "Dunno, lemme see."

She sang a handful of scales, and with each note, a brilliant burst of rainbow-colored light exploded before her.

"Nope, I'm one hundred percent," Emily said.

Paige looked to Kevin and Cassie. The beautiful object of Kevin's every desire was looking at him as if through new eyes—new eyes that liked what they saw. Cassie finally knew the truth about Ryan's duplicity and Kevin's true love for her. Cassie felt a warmth rise up from her heart as she gazed at Kevin and finally realized that she loved him too.

"You know?" Paige whispered to her sisters. "All in all, this has been one truly awesome weekend!"

Epilogue

The house was quiet—but still so much more alive than an ordinary house—as the Charmed Ones and Emily led Kevin and Cassie through it, to the lush, spacious grounds beyond. Phoebe could sense the renewed positive energy that permeated its long, winding halls; a pulse of excitement thrummed through its walls, floors, and ceilings. This was a house that would never—*could* never—die. Even if it were reduced to rubble, its every brick and stone would retain its power, spreading its magic and wonder to whatever places its remains would be used to construct.

They found the rest of the party guests mulling around, dazed and confused, near a great fountain. Ryan was muttering angrily to himself; Craig looked like a lost child. Several of the partyers froze in alarm at the sight of the Charmed Ones.

"Okay, ladies, you know what we need to

do," Piper said as she raised her hands.

"Wait!" pleaded Kevin. "You're about to cast some kind of spell, aren't you? One that will make everyone forget about what happened here?"

Kevin and Cassie clung tightly to each other.

"We don't want to forget," Cassie pleaded.

Phoebe grinned. "Don't worry. We'll make sure you remember the good parts. It's just, y'know, that pesky magic stuff that's got to go."

"What you'll forget are ghosts and demons. You'll remember all the moments that matter," Paige said, sighing with longing as she looked at the luscious Craig.

"Then we'll still be together?" Kevin asked, his hand clasped with that of his sweetheart, Cassie. "We won't forget that we finally found each other?"

"You'll be fine," Piper assured them.

Kevin and Cassie took their places with the others, most of whom were still too out of it to object or to truly even question as the Charmed Ones chanted and emerald and crimson rings settled over them, spiraling and spinning until they turned clear and vanished.

"You!" cried Ryan, storming toward Kevin. "You think you can just take something that's mine? Cassie and I are getting married, and there's not a blasted thing you can do about it. Now get your hands off her and—"

Cassie detached herself from Kevin so

quickly that Kevin never had a chance to say a word in his own defense. Her fist flew in a blur at Ryan's stubbly jaw and met with a high, sharp *crack*. Ryan flopped over backward, the tails of his designer jacket whipping out like great dark wings, and he splashed down into a muddy puddle, sputtering and cursing up a storm. But he did not go near either Kevin or Cassie again.

"Whoa," said Kevin, smiling ear to ear, "maybe I should put a boxing ring in the house. Never know when I might need you coming to my rescue again, and I wouldn't want you losing your edge."

She hugged him tight. "I think there's something else I'd rather be practicing," she said, before planting a big one on him.

With a laugh, he scooped his beloved giggling Cassie up into his arms and carried her back into the house.

When Phoebe looked back to the guests, she saw them happily chatting and laughing about the awesome time they'd had over the weekend. It was clear from the snippets of conversation she heard as they filed toward the gates that each one had vague memories of the ghost's shenanigans, but they genuinely believed Kevin (and a small army of special effects and stunt guys) had been behind all of it. Only Ryan slumped along sullenly, his mood black until Tamara surprisingly raced to his side and took his mud-stained arm.

"You know, I think that whole 'romantic love' thing is bogus, right? So this Mrs. Tobias gig," she said quickly, "does it come with a 401(k)?"

Ryan shot a glance back to Karl, who had been talking to Tamara a moment ago. Karl shrugged and went off to his own car.

"Wow," Paige said. "Married to Tamara. Ryan's a pretty bad guy, but I'm not sure even he deserves that!"

Phoebe nodded. "I am!"

Only Craig remained at the gates when all the others had gone, though from his confused look it seemed apparent that even he did not know what he was waiting for. At last, he turned and left the grounds.

Paige's heart sank as she watched him go. Damn, he was a hottie! Oh, well, maybe another time . . .

"Wishing you'd gotten his number?" teased Piper.

"Don't worry," added Phoebe. "He's got yours."

Paige's brow crinkled in confusion. "But I never gave him my phone—" Then she got it. "Oh. He got my number as in he knows I'm interested in him. Funny, funny, har-har. I was a good girl!"

"Yes, you were, we're sorry," Phoebe said. She turned to Piper. "Aren't we?"

"Well . . . ," Piper muttered. Phoebe's elbow nearly found Piper's ribs. "Okay, okay!"

Piper yelped. "Yep, sorry, that's me. Yikes . . ."

An emerald shimmer sprang up before the Charmed Ones, and the spirit of Robert Maxwell appeared. Emily's face lit up at the sight of him.

"I thought it best to wait until all the curious eyes had turned away," he said softly. "Discretion, valor, all that."

"Missed you," Emily whispered, almost too softly to be heard by anyone but Paige, who stood beside her.

The spirit of Robert Maxwell turned to the Charmed Ones. "I apologize for not coming to your rescue sooner. I've played many a hero . . . but being a true hero didn't come naturally to me. I wonder if I should abandon acting altogether or if my days as a haunting spirit should continue. Haunting houses is fun, after all. . . ."

"I dunno," Phoebe said to the ghost. "It takes a lot of courage to overcome your fears and to stop worrying about what other people think of you, which is what you did. Do you *really* want to continue pretending to be someone you're not?"

Maxwell looked away—then fixed his gaze on Emily, the witch who had given him this smashing second life. "I suppose I owe you an explanation," he said, speaking to the Charmed Ones, though he could not take his eyes off the lovely Emily. "When I was fighting the demon and all seemed lost, I realized that something had happened to weaken the spell binding me to the house. I was free to go anywhere I wished, even to my final peaceful reward, if that was what I desired. Instead, I went to Emily, and brought her back to help the Charmed Ones."

"So you were a hero," Paige said. "I knew it all along!"

"No, Phoebe was right. All those years, I was afraid . . . ," the ghost admitted as he reached out and stroked Emily's lovely hair. "Afraid of being forgotten. That's why you did it, isn't it? Because you heard me with old Doc Phillips that day, when I told him the fears that kept me up at night."

Emily nodded, her eyes brimming with tears.

"Then what you did wasn't *really* a selfish act," Paige said. "Magic shouldn't punish you."

The ghost smiled at Paige. "What's done is done. The only way she'll be free now is if the spell she cast is reversed. Let me tell it to you."

Emily rushed forward and stopped him. She said, "You're not scared anymore . . . but are you really ready to move on?"

Maxell grinned. "Well . . ."

"Me too. Maybe living forever wouldn't be so bad," Emily told him, "if I didn't have to go through it alone."

Nodding, Maxwell snapped his fingers and a ghostly horse appeared. "I always wanted to do a Western," he admitted. He helped Emily onto the horse, and the immortal witch and the Hollywood ghost rode off into the sunset.

"Well, whaddya know?" asked Phoebe. "We get a happy ending after all!"

Paige heard the crunch of gravel behind her. She whirled to find herself staring into Craig's handsome, chiseled face.

"Y'know, I kept thinking I was forgetting something," he told her.

"Oh?" she said, her heart fit to explode at the sight of him. "What's that?"

He smiled—and kissed her, his lips blazing, his hands bold and strong as he took her into his arms. She melted into his kiss.

When she finally came up for air, she fanned herself with one hand and told her sisters, "Now *that's* magic!"

"I was wondering if you wanted to come see my club," Craig offered, gazing deeply into Paige's liquid eyes. "It's a comedy club . . . should be good for a laugh and, who knows. Maybe something more."

Paige's smile was radiant as she quickly nodded. "Uh-*huh*."

All four walked to the gates together, Paige splitting from her sisters as she followed Craig to his Humvee. *You should always just be yourself and not worry about what others think*, Paige realized. *That's what the ghost took almost a century to learn. And it's what I've always known. . . .*

Laughing, Phoebe called, "Here we go again!"

"Yeah!" added Piper in a teasing voice. "One

weekend of no hot guys. Just one. I knew you couldn't do it. I told you so!"

For some reason, Paige just wasn't listening. Not even when her sisters burst into good-natured laughter and headed off to the car so they could ride off into the sunset too.

About the Author

Scott Ciencin is a *New York Times* bestselling author of more than seventy books from Simon & Schuster, HarperCollins, Scholastic, and many more. He has written Charmed: *Luck Be a Lady* and *Light of the World*, Buffy the Vampire Slayer: *Sweet Sixteen*, and co-written Angel: *Nemesis* and the Angel short story "It Could Happen to You" with his wife. He has worked on the *Jurassic Park*, *Star Wars*, *Transformers*, and *Dinotopia* franchises, written for Marvel and DC Comics, and is the author of the popular Vampire Odyssey and Dinoverse (which has been optioned as a feature film) series. He is also the writer of *Everquest: The Rogue's Hour* and the *Silent Hill* comics based on the bestselling horror video game and motion picture. He lives in Sarasota, Florida, with his beloved wife, Denise.